NB 8901719 6

D0333960

EDUCATION AUTHORITY NE REGION
WITHDRAWN FROM STOCK

THE OUTCASTS

Also by L.S. Matthews:

WINNER OF THE FIDLER AWARD
SHORTLISTED FOR THE
BRANFORD BOASE AWARD
Fish

Other titles available from Hodder Children's Books:

The Ice-Boy
Murkmere
Patricia Elliott

Step into the Dark
Feast of Fools
Ship's Angel
Bridget Crowley

CHERUB: The Recruit
CHERUB: Class A
Robert Muchamore

THE OUTCASTS

L. S. Matthews

Hodder Children's Books

A division of Hodder Headline Limited

To all of my family, past and present.

To the young people of whom too much has been
demanded, and of whom nothing is expected.

And to the dimension shifters —
don't worry, your secret is safe. After all,
this is simply a work of fiction —
no one would believe it, would they?

North Eastern Education and Library Board		
NESSEC		
NB 590139 6		
Askews & Holts	29-Oct-2015	
	£5.99	

CHAPTER ONE

Joe came across Iz on his way to Maths first thing on Monday morning.

He had been looking for his friend, but now he hung back for a moment, because he knew Iz well enough to see he was up to something, and Joe didn't want to be caught up in it.

If there was trouble, Joe always seemed to be caught up in it, and, generally speaking, Iz was trouble. It fizzed from him in little blue lightnings Joe almost felt he could see. And it was very important right now that Joe did not get into trouble.

Joe stopped for a moment and eyed up Iz, who was gangling his thin, wiry frame into some kind of impossible sitting position on the high, narrow windowsill in the corridor. Screwing his top half sideways, his dark fringe flopped over his face, he seemed to be writing something. As few teachers ever succeeded in getting Iz to pick up a pen, this, in itself, was suspicious.

Two sixth formers were standing looking out of the window next to him. One of them – pale, medium-scrawny, with badly formed dreadlocks – called something to two girls down below in the quad.

Joe hardly had a moment to take this in. A fast-flowing river of students appeared behind him and swept towards him. When the first body collided with him, his bag took the brunt, and he barely staggered. Joe was a solid, square-shaped boy, somehow also round, and when he stopped, it was likely to create an impression in a narrow corridor full of stampeding fellow students.

Iz jumped down from the sill when he saw the pile-up of pupils getting interesting.

Joe, with his short, dark hair unruffled, stood gazing at him thoughtfully, saying 'Oof,' at regular intervals as another boy cannoned into the scrimmage massing at his back. Further down the corridor, girls were now coming across the blockage of boys pushing and jostling each other. The girls stood back for a moment, then started protesting loudly that they could not pass through. One of the boys in front, trying to swing his bag at a neighbour, accidentally clipped a girl with a ponytail of long, golden curls.

She flashed her large, beautiful blue eyes, swore loudly above all the noise in the corridor, and drew back her arm to strike.

In the distance, through the moshpit, Iz could see a pale jacket and a shining forehead approaching.

'Move, Joe,' he said, stretching out an arm and sweeping the larger boy alongside him before marching swiftly along the corridor. The dam removed, the river of students flowed behind, around and in front of them once more.

'What's that?' Joe asked suspiciously, as Iz flourished a scrappy piece of white paper ahead of him. Iz did not answer but darted forward suddenly, between two girls, and lightly touched the paper on to the jacket of the dreadlocked sixth former, who was now in front of them. Wary of reading, Joe could still make out the words in black pen: 'PLEASE COMB ME'.

He sighed.

'Iz, did you hear about the trip?'

'No, what trip?' asked Iz, but his eyes were not on Joe. He was carefully pulling at the key ring attached to the bag of the girl to one side of him. This successfully undid the zip, so that in a flash, Iz had her pencil case out of the bag. In only one more flash, he was doubled up on the floor with his hands around his head for protection.

Joe stood back again, this time avoiding chaos by backing against the wall, until the girl, with long, dark hair flying, had decided to stop hitting Iz with the pencil case in case she damaged any of its contents, and flounced off triumphantly.

Iz straightened up, laughing.

'What trip?'

'Weren't you at registration?' said Joe, peevishly.

'I never go to registration,' said Iz.

'Why? We all have to go,' said Joe. 'Well, if you'd been there, you'd have heard – that trip they asked us about ages ago, remember? We put our names down. Well, we've been picked out of the hat to go. Us! But we have to stay out of trouble – or we'll lose our places.'

'Oh!' said Iz, for once lost for words.

There were lots of questions queuing up in his head, but at the moment, he couldn't get over the fact he'd been chosen. He never got to go on trips – not even trips where there wasn't a limit on places. Staff didn't want to take boys like him. They never said so. There was always a reason – it was easy enough to find one. He was always temporarily excluded just as the trip was due, or something. He hadn't been on a trip since he was little.

In the classroom, Iz took his place next to Joe, strangely quiet. He was torn between excitement and anxiety. Part of him was prepared for disappointment. It wouldn't come off, there was bound to be a catch. He couldn't even bear to ask Joe for more details.

Their teacher, a young woman still in training, noticed Iz's quietness and wondered at it. She would have liked Iz if she had not had to try to teach him.

*

Further along the corridor, the news of the trip was having a very different effect on the girl with the long golden hair.

'God, it's so brilliant, I can't believe I'm going,' she confided to her neighbour, her large blue eyes flashing excitedly.

Unfortunately, always loud, her version of a whisper was clearly audible. It was the last straw for the ageing, tired Mr Roberts who was in the middle of a complicated explanation of probability.

'That's it, Helen, I've warned you twice. Out, and no discussion please.'

Other, more discreet whisperers stopped abruptly. To everyone's surprise, Helen rose meekly and walked out of the room with only the trace of a flounce and closed the door quietly behind her. Mr Roberts was used to battle with Helen at such moments; he hadn't really expected the 'no discussion' to work. Surprised and pleased at this unexplained success, he turned back to the class and continued.

Helen stood sadly outside the room. Hopefully she hadn't blown it. The tutor had said they had to stay out of trouble to keep their place on the trip. This wasn't really trouble, in Helen's terms. Normally, she would get in a row and they would send for one of the high-up teachers, and she would get a detention or something. But she couldn't be sure – the school's idea of 'trouble' had always been very different to her own and was still slightly puzzling to her.

'Helen?'

Mr Roberts had appeared, and was looking at her warily. The volume from the classroom had increased the second he had stepped out of the door, but Helen, wrapped up in her torment, hadn't noticed.

Mr Roberts was doing the proper thing, of course, Helen realised. They weren't supposed to leave you standing out here all lesson, one of the Learning Support ladies had told her. But some of them did. Mr Roberts always came to tell you off properly and send you back in to try again. She remembered that he had done that with other people. He hadn't actually had the chance with her, she realised, because she'd either had to be collected and taken off to someone's office because she'd blown her top, or she'd run off in a fury, to be caught later.

'I'm sorry to have to put you out like that, Helen, but I had warned you twice,' he began.

'Other people were talking,' said Helen, in a pale return to form, but with little defiance in her voice.

'Probably, but not so loudly as you. Nor so persistently

once I'd warned them,' said Mr Roberts. There was a pause. Helen wondered if she was supposed to say something.

'Shall I stay here or can I go back in, then?' she said irritably.

The teacher eyed her curiously. What had got into the girl? He wasn't sure, but he wasn't going to knock it.

Sensing he somehow had the upper hand, he cleared his throat.

'You are welcome back in the classroom, Helen, so long as you don't continue to disrupt my lesson—' he began.

Helen recognised that he was 'going all formal on her'. It was best to interrupt them when they did that, or you could be in for a lecture lasting all day.

'No - detention or anything?'

Mr Roberts was taken aback.

'Of course not. So long as we carry on all right till the end of the period.'

He'd never known the girl to be bothered about detention before - up until now, it had singularly failed as a sanction. In fact, she usually failed to turn up for the sessions.

He noticed the biting of the lip, the furious concentration on a peeling streak of nail varnish. In spite of himself, and the growing din from the room behind him, he heard himself ask:

'Are you all right, Helen? I mean—'

'It's just this trip!' the girl blurted out, tossing back her hair and looking up at him with eyes at once tearful and angry. 'I got picked to go on this trip, for a whole week, but I mustn't get into any trouble, and—'

'Oh!' interrupted Mr Roberts suddenly, and Helen

stopped, surprised at the note of revelati

'Of course, the trip. Yes, they said someth
briefing. That sounds marvellous, Helen.'

She looked at him, confused again by the note in his
voice, this time of warm amusement.

'But this won't mean I've blown it, will it?'

'No, no, really, you handled leaving the room very well,'
continued Mr Roberts encouragingly. 'Hurry up back in
now, so we don't waste any more time.' And he followed her
back into the classroom, quelling the noise with his famously
loud 'Uh, hum!' which had worked for him for thirty years.

*

Over in the Learning Support room, Mia was being greeted
enthusiastically by Mrs Johnson, who was in charge. A lady
of about middle age, with dark hair which might have been
curly had it not had the nonsense chopped short before it
could start, she beamed with apparent kindness, but she
could be sharp, Mia knew, with those eyes of hers, the eyes
of the predator.

'Well, Mia, how about this trip then? Are you looking
forward to going?'

Mia walked straight past her as if she were not there, to
the desk where she always sat, and thumped her bag on the
floor.

'Now, now, Mia, we know better than that,' came Mrs
Johnson's voice, kindly on the outside, but with that touch
of steel coming into it now, Mia could tell. She stared straight
ahead, waiting for the woman who always worked with her,
but was aware of the figure of Mrs Johnson: smooth smart
clothes, jingly jewellery, unnecessary.

..., eye contact. Let's try it again,'
... in the voice she'd consciously
...ouraging, warm, yet firm.

...iscordant fluting, a mean wind hooting
...pipes. She stiffened, readying herself for
...ts of old, but suddenly, there was a familiar
br... ...pe at the corner of her eye, a clean smell. Then
the gen... ...ound of Miss Ermine's voice.

'Sorry I'm a bit late, Mrs Johnson, Mia; I got caught up in
an incident on the way along the Maths corridor.'

Mia noted the apology; knew without looking that Miss
Ermine had not looked at her as she spoke.

Mrs Johnson forgot Mia for the moment.

'An incident? Not one of ours I hope.' By ours, Mia
thought, she means the people who aren't 'right', who get
trapped in here.

'No, for once. Those silly sixth formers, can you believe it.
I wouldn't normally intervene, but all these girls were
clambering over one of the boys . . .'

Mrs Johnson drew in her breath and looked scandalised.
Seeing she was about to embark on one of her favourite
topics – the Outrageously Lewd Behaviour of some students
– Miss Ermine managed to head her off.

'Not like that, not that at all,' she said quickly, 'I was going
to ignore it but I heard shouts of real pain. Underneath was
Martin, and those silly girls had been at him with combs.
One of them was completely entangled. I've left him at sick
bay. I'm afraid it'll have to be cut out.'

The colours of Mrs Johnson faded out of Mia's view; a
black sky lifted from above her shoulders. Miss Ermine sat

down, and with no more ado, no small talk, placed books in front of Mia. Explanation was kept to a minimum – there was no need now for Miss Ermine to say, 'I won't help you unless you want me to.' They had met, a year ago, and the lines of their working together had been drawn out then, simply, by Miss Ermine. She didn't go on and repeat everything or say it eight different ways, as if you were thick.

Now, Mia had her table, her books and the correct person at her side. She picked up the right sort of pen. She pushed away the uncomfortable thought that Miss Ermine was part of the necessary set-up which made her comfort zone complete. Things, it was usually, not people. Mia had felt a twinge of panic when Miss Ermine had been unexpectedly late. Once, she had been off ill for a day. It had not been a very good day for Mia, or for some of the school staff. Mia pushed the feeling aside. Mia didn't 'do' people.

Miss Ermine's voice came calm and low from Mia's left side. It was unusual for her to speak out of the blue like this. Mia could hear the speaker's discomfort at having to intrude, though she tried to hide it and sound matter-of-fact.

'I know about the trip, Mia. I really think you will enjoy it. I'm going along, you know.'

Everyone had been congratulating her about the trip. She *was* excited and pleased, mostly. But then she'd felt the fear, the fear that things wouldn't be right. It was very hard for the rest of the world to be right for Mia, she had realised. It put people out, they could get cross and unhappy. And that, she had been told, was a bad thing, and generally she'd found it was. Bad for them, bad for her.

But Miss Ermine was coming.

Twice, Miss Ermine had been honoured by a smile, when Mia appeared to forget that she didn't. Smile. Mrs Johnson would have said, 'That's great, Mia. Smile! You see, everyone, I've made a breakthrough!'

Miss Ermine hadn't acted as if it was anything other than normal. And so neither had Mia.

Now she turned and looked at Miss Ermine.

Mia had a glance which you couldn't catch hold of; often she did not seem to turn her eyes towards the thing she was really looking at. When you caught a glimpse of those eyes, it was like seeing a flash of the sea. But now she turned them straight on to Miss Ermine's eyes, and Miss Ermine caught her breath as she stared through two tiny portholes at a great, wild, unfixed ocean, as big as an ocean can be, blue-grey, dangerous, a swallower of ships and sailors, a treasure-chest of strange and unknown, beautiful and terrible things at great depths; how could one person, let alone a small girl, hold such a thing, and not go mad with the keeping of it?

'That's good,' said Mia, in her monotone, and Miss Ermine acknowledged her with a little nod of the head, while inside she seized and hugged the moment.

*

Back in the Maths corridor, the top set was getting to grips with cosine, sine and tangent.

Chris was being jabbed in the ribs by his neighbour, Charlie.

'Good us getting on the trip. But what about the others going, have you heard?'

'Bloody hell, yeah, I know, that weirdo girl and half the other spoons in the school—'

'Chris Winter, what was I just saying?' Mrs Pierce was renowned for the voice which went with the name.

'I . . .' began Chris. He was a very clever, very able boy. Hence he was good at being able to talk, listen to a friend, and still have half an ear turned to the teacher. But for God's sake, what on earth had she been on about?

'Perhaps you'd like to give me your answer to question 3a, as I asked?' prompted the teacher. Chris looked quickly at his book and read out his answer confidently. It was right, of course. It always was.

CHAPTER TWO

It was impossible for people like Iz to stay out of trouble for two weeks or even more than a day, thought Joe gloomily. Almost two weeks had passed since the day their inclusion on the trip had been announced. Joe had been in agony almost every school day since.

He was not too worried about his own ability to get through the time without serious problems. Things had been a lot better lately, compared with when he'd first started this school, and had tried ducking out of lessons, pleading headaches, trying to get toilet breaks. He was embarrassed when he remembered. And people were pleased with him – his mum, especially, because she couldn't have any worries, not when it already took all her time to sit and worry, all day, sometimes all night, with a drink and some pills.

She worried so hard that it meant there was no time to cook or wash up or sort out Joe's clothes, or do the shopping – she couldn't even leave the house now. Joe supposed that if she did, the worry would wait back at the house for her, and while she was out and not minding it, it would get bigger and bigger till it was out of control when she got back.

So Joe was pleased that he was getting on at school with less hassle. He was just disappointed that the things he hated at school – writing, reading, Maths, PE (that covered pretty well every lesson) – he still hated and dreaded. He should have felt better that he was behaving himself, being more grown-up. But a small part of him seemed to feel he hadn't grown up, just given in. To make everyone's life easier. But not necessarily his.

Iz, Joe thought, waiting outside the Deputy Head's office, Iz was very different. He really didn't seem to be able to help himself. And to be fair, some teachers didn't exactly make things easy.

Joe had suffered agonies, because he was terrified of going on the trip alone – or rather, without Iz.

He was sure Iz had blown it twice in particular: once when he marched into every lesson with a pair of Science goggles on his head and insisted to irritated teachers that he had to keep them on for Health and Safety reasons; once when he'd dodged a fist which had then hit the fire alarm and got the whole school out. Somehow, despite lots of angry words, Iz had not lost his place on the trip. And now, here, with success close at hand, Iz had probably gone and done it, after a huge row with Mr Frost, the old, fierce and unfriendly English teacher.

Iz, sitting drooping in the Deputy Head's office, was feeling possibly worse than his friend fretting outside.

He had gone from blinding rage, to storming off, to coming back to the high-up who'd come to collect him (and who could really be quite decent), to pacing and explaining angrily how in the right he was. But somewhere in this mess, he knew he was at fault again.

The Deputy Head, a small but awesome lady with a metallic helmet of hair and heels you could hear coming for miles, stared calmly at Iz. When in her office, she had never seen Iz other than defiant, angry. At other times he had been leaping, climbing, falling or punching. She cleared her throat.

'I'll read through the details Mr Frost has provided. He says that immediately on entering the classroom, you kicked someone's chair and bag, then hurled abuse at him and he told you to stand outside.' The Deputy Head paused, surprised that there had been no interruption from the captive with his version of events. Iz had his head down, sitting on the edge of the padded office chair, looking at the floor.

'Look at me please, Iz,' said the Deputy Head without particular feeling. She noted that the hands with smudged biro tattoos were shaking. To her surprise, when Iz looked up, his dog eyes were distinctly shinier than usual.

'Is that what happened? And if so, can you explain why?' she continued.

Iz said in a bored, hopeless monotone, 'I walked into the room. I tripped over something and fell on to the chair. It hurt. I got up and saw it was Pearson's bag he'd left right out in the bloody doorway – sorry,' – at a *tch* sound from Miss Metalhead – '*damn* doorway, and so I kicked it back out the way and told him not to be such an ar–' Iz stopped again at a look from the woman opposite, writing as he spoke.

'You told him not to be so thoughtless, yes,' she said encouragingly.

'Yes, then Mr Frost just screamed at me, "Get Out". Just like that. I couldn't even explain. So I did. Get out I mean.'

'You don't think Mr Frost might have been speaking to you – or trying to get your attention – at any point during the time you fell over or kicked the bag, do you?'

'No!' Iz looked surprised. Then thought. 'I didn't hear him anyway, if he did.'

'And what's this bit about hurling abuse at him?'

'I didn't! I shouted at Pearson and called him a—'

Again, Miss Metalhead held up a hand to stem the flow. She sighed. She knew Iz of old. She found it highly likely that Iz's story and Mr Frost's were both true to an extent.

'Well, Iz, I'll have a word with Mr Frost and see what he wants to do about it. Maybe an apology, maybe a detention will do it. But if it's detention, it will have to be deferred, because you've got this trip coming next week, haven't you? Mind you, be careful – we won't have forgotten this. I take behaviour of this kind very seriously.'

Iz was hardly listening now. He was trying to keep up with her. The trip? He could still go? It was so unbelievable that he nearly gave it away. Nearly stood up, leapt about and thanked her. Steady now, Iz, play it cool. She knows this is a real let-off-the-hook. She's having to sound very threatening, to keep pride. Look impressed. Look cowed. That is what is required.

Iz stifled his start of surprise almost well enough for the Deputy Head not to notice. He kept his head low, his eyes down as he shook her hand and headed for the door, freedom and Joe; and the trip still waiting, still his.

The Deputy Head, passing into the Main Office, saw the pair hugging and punching each other as they disappeared towards the last lesson of the day.

Mia had had her own appointment in the same office on the same day. Miss Ermine had finally managed to track her down, hiding at the top of one of the outside fire escapes, rocking in a small ball, and had somehow enticed her into the Deputy Head's room in a calmer state of mind.

If the lady with the shiny, solid hair found it a difficult interview, Mia didn't seem to notice or care. She kept up her familiar, high-pitched hum, and stared, apparently fascinated, at the dust motes which whirled in the sunlight through the side window.

With the aid of Miss Ermine, who had been walking along the corridor just behind Mia, it was ascertained that the girl had leapt on another, seizing hair; but from then on, it appeared to be half-a-dozen of one and six of the other, as the Deputy Head liked to call it – that is, the other student had engaged in the fight just as vigorously. No one appeared to have been hurt, but the school was wary of the other student's parents. She had told tales before, always from her own angle, and caused all sorts of trouble from that quarter.

The Deputy Head gave up interrogating Mia directly, and turned to Miss Ermine, almost hopelessly.

'And do we have any idea what caused this rather violent reaction?'

The voice came, unexpectedly, from the mote-gazer's chair.

'She called me a flipping spoon.'

The words were delivered one by one, on the same note, in the slightly foreign-sounding accent that no one could quite place.

The Deputy Head paused for a moment, surprised, pleased

at least, that the child had answered. And realised that this was so unusual, it must matter deeply.

The Deputy Head looked between Mia and Miss Ermine, not sure who to address.

'A spoon? And that is, er . . . ?'

'Stupid. Thick. Weirdo,' said Mia, 'she said those things too.'

Miss Ermine said quietly, 'I did actually hear that. You see, I was walking behind Mia but must have been obscured by one of the pillars. I don't think the other girl was aware of me when she spoke.'

'Well, Mia,' said the Deputy Head, pulling her chest up and out, 'you know you have worked very hard on your social skills, and you must keep trying. We can't have students going around hitting each other all the time, it's not the correct response to taunts. However, we also cannot have this sort of name-calling. It's very unkind and is still bullying, when all's said and done, in the eyes of the school.'

Mia wondered where the eyes of the school were. Perhaps the big windows. Maybe hidden. She drew her shoulders in a little, afraid.

'Don't worry, Mia,' said the shiny-haired lady, softening her rooster posture, misreading Mia's cowering.

She turned to Miss Ermine.

'I hope, in time, Mia will learn to ignore such people. After all, everyone knows Mia is none of those things. A very able girl, very able indeed. I'll handle this with the other girl's parents. They seem to be very well versed in the correct practice for bullying issues. We cannot have the school's policy on inclusion jeopardised by silly ignorance.'

Miss Ermine smiled, and a little sigh of relief escaped her.

'If that's all? I'll go with Mia on to English,' she said cautiously.

'Absolutely. We don't want Mia interrupted in her studies,' said the Deputy Head, looking at Mia who had risen automatically from her chair and come to stand at Miss Ermine's side.

'Best behaviour from now on, Mia. And enjoy the trip next week, both of you . . .' and they were firmly ushered out of the door.

CHAPTER THREE

There were only twenty students going on the trip, so Mr Evans, the PE teacher, would take the majority in the school minibus with Miss Ermine.

Mr Taylor would drive his own car with his wife, who taught Science, and the remaining students – Iz, Joe and Chris Winter – in the back, as they couldn't split Iz and Joe, and could not bear the thought of them together amongst other inflammatory characters on the minibus. They hoped they had found the best solution possible. In Mr Evans' ideal world, Iz would have been transported alone in the back of a sealed container lorry.

*

In the separate households, the selected students were starting to feel surges of excitement. Preparations had to be made; there was a list of kit from school. Walking boots, wash stuff, underwear . . .

Mia's mother went shopping for it all, trying to hide her pleasure and anxiety from her daughter. Her dad helped her pack, tried to stop smiling all the time. For the first time, there were phone calls between them and Miss Ermine.

Mia's mum was very big and round now, because the baby was due any day. Dad had joined the worriers about how Mia would react. He told Mum that he had read about someone like Mia putting a tripwire on the stairs to see what happened when their toddler brother fell down, because they didn't understand about people. Mum insisted that Mia would be all right, that it would be good for her. But she hoped too for some signs that her daughter would be less needy, would find her own life. The trip was a big step. They hoped it would be forwards.

*

Chris's mum took the list from his bag, where she always searched for school letters. She bought everything they hadn't got already, which wasn't much. She then hurried around the house, seeking out odd items to pack.

'It says a light, waterproof coat. Where's that expensive kagoul thing we bought for holiday last year, Chris?' she pleaded in vain. Chris called out the customary answer from his station at the computer, where he was gaming furiously. 'Uh, sorry, don't know.'

*

Helen took money her mother gave her and went out to meet her dad, who was on a rare visit and had offered to drive her in to the nearest big town to do her shopping. She would rather have gone with her best mate, but she knew it was a chance she couldn't miss, to go with her dad – he would always be generous with extra money on top of what Mum had given her. She enjoyed shopping. She bought her own versions of what was asked for on the list, ignoring the rain-proof jacket and deciding to take her leather one. 'Several short-sleeved T-shirts,' she read. She thought for a moment, then headed past the racks towards the long-sleeved ones. She always kept her arms covered.

'Will you be long, now?' asked her dad.

'No, not long,' said Helen. 'I have to do the ironing still when I get back home, and I've all the lunches to pack.'

Helen was amazed she was getting to go on this trip. She often had so much work to do looking after her half-brothers and -sisters that she didn't even get out to go to school for weeks at a time. This trip would be a real holiday.

*

Joe's mother would have a carer coming in more often, and a friend from down the road. Joe had been taken out by one of the kind staff at school who helped out in the Learning Support room, with the list and special money for everything from the school. She offered to pack all the things in a case for him, which she'd give to Mr Evans beforehand.

Joe tried to keep his leaving casual, quiet, like it was a normal going-to-school day. He didn't think his mum noticed. He shut the door behind him and ran across the road and down the hill a little, where his little sister stood waiting to kiss him goodbye outside the foster carer's home. They were lucky to have found someone so close by, but still Joe missed her, for all her annoying ways.

*

Iz had handed his mum the list, and she had snatched it sulkily.

'I thought this was free. Now what do they want? Always bloody money.'

Iz's dad butted in from the sink, where he was piling up

dirty dishes in the way of a helpful man who never washes up. He was visiting, which was rare but stressful nonetheless. Mum had had yet another bust-up with sort-of stepdad number six, so at least there were just the three of them to argue. This time, as always, Mum insisted it was 'final', but Iz had no doubt he'd be re-installed comfortably by the time he returned from the trip, worst luck.

'No such thing as free,' his dad said loudly above the clatter. 'Waste of time, the whole thing. School trips! What'll that teach you about the building trade? Eh?'

Iz's mum, on hearing this from her ex-husband, perversely flicked out the list and narrowed her eyes.

'Well, let's have a look, anyway. You missed out on some trips, didn't you? I don't see why all these other kids get to go all the time. I suppose everyone else will have this stuff . . .'

'Yeah, of course they will. You don't have to have walking boots, Mr Taylor says. He says you can have leather trainers. I'd rather have them.'

'And I suppose everyone else will have them, and they'll all be Nike or whatever?' put in his dad in a knowing, mocking tone, continuing above Iz's noisy denials, 'And CD players? And computer games?'

'Cut it out, the both of you,' shouted his mum, above the din. 'I'll get what's needed and nothing more. If you're going to go, you'd better do it properly. But don't let us down now, Iz. No complaints from school, no phone calls from Mr Bloody Taylor. Your dad doesn't want to go driving all over the country just to pick you up because they can't manage.'

CHAPTER FOUR

On the Saturday after school had broken up for half-term, Mr Evans and Mr Taylor drew their vehicles out of the school car park, laden with excited travellers. It was a long, tiring, hot journey down the country, deep into the ancient, softened green of the South West.

In Mr Taylor's car, the trip had been fairly quiet. Chris Winter, sulking slightly at having been kept away from his friend Charlie and crushed into a Mondeo with that irritating git Iz, and Joe, who took up two seats, seemed to repress the other two with his mood.

Iz started getting twitchy late on in the journey.

'Are we there, Mrs Taylor? Where are we going again?'

'Well, we are in Dorset at last, Iz, and the house is on the Dorset/Devon border, it says here. Can't be far now.'

The last part of the journey, though short, was the most tiring for driver, navigator and passengers in Mr Taylor's car, which had long ago overtaken and lost the minibus. The roads became more winding; the hedge banks steeper and more green.

The oaks and other trees which were left to tower in the

hedges were old, old. The thick green of verge and bank seemed to be left untouched, untamed; myriads of different forms of leaf seemed to fight for every bit of space. When there were glimpses of land through a gateway in the hedge, or great, smooth hills rising up suddenly above the road, even the turf somehow looked ancient. Occasionally, the hillsides were covered in strange ripples, heavily shadowed, or sudden craters and perfectly smooth circular humps.

To the younger passengers, this all just looked excitingly different. They did not know why, and did not stare and wonder at the strange wildflowers flourishing showily from the sides of the road, but they did know that they liked the feel of this new part of their world.

Iz caught sight of a really noticeable array of round humps on the flank of one of the hills. Again, he felt the oldness of the land, though he would not have been able to say why; he was not used to seeing fields with streams just being allowed to meander through and trees left standing around in the middle, as they had always done. Yet though the humps and occasional crater were furred with the same tight, bright turf that looked as if it had been there for ever, they looked as though they could not be natural – and maybe those strange ripples couldn't be either.

'Did they have alien spacecraft landing here once or something, Mr Taylor?' he asked, leaning forward and causing Joe and Chris to wriggle uncomfortably, as they were rather squashed. Many members of staff would have cited this as an example of Iz's silly questions, but Mr Taylor merely said:

'What makes you ask that?'

'There are flipping big lump things on some of the hills and back there, there was like, a brilliant crater. Or was it bombs in the War?'

Iz was one of those people that like to ask a question and then try and answer it themselves. Mr Taylor waited to check whether Iz was really interested, or whether he was going to invent an explanation involving extra-terrestrials and World War 2 anti-aircraft guns battling it out for this key metropolis of rural Dorset, but he was rewarded by an expectant silence from the back seat.

'Iron Age burial mounds, some of them. There are lots down here. The ripples are where the land was ploughed long ago and hasn't been touched since. Some are terraces where the Romans tried to grow grape vines.'

'Oh,' said Iz. There was a pause. 'I was keeping an eye out for one of those big black panther things they say has been seen round here. One of the lads told me. Should be a pretty exciting place, what with that and the skull in the house and everything.'

'Yes,' said Mr Taylor, 'but I wouldn't get your hopes up about the panther. I notice people always see them just when they really don't want to, and when the whole army goes out to find one, they never can.'

'Does the skull really scream?' asked Joe. Iz had read out to him the story of the house's screaming skull from the leaflet they'd had about the trip.

'I don't know. I think that might be folklore, Joe,' said Mr Taylor.

'And if it ever leaves the house, a disaster will happen,' said Joe confidently.

'I think that's really a bit of superstitious nonsense, Joe,' put in Mrs Taylor.

'Yeah, I suppose it's a good story, and it stops people trying to nick the skull or something,' put in Chris from the back.

'Or it might want to make you nick the skull, if you were an enemy,' said Iz.

'True,' said Chris, and the two boys seemed to make a surprising truce for the moment.

Suddenly the car dived, out of the sun and the views, down, down into a tunnel of dark mossy green, where the trees formed an arched leafy roof that plunged the narrow road into flickering shadow as they wound downhill, with occasional splashes of emerald where the sun managed to hit a hole in the canopy.

The temperature inside the car plummeted instantly by several degrees. The travellers sighed with relief at the creeping cool and drank in the damp smell of earth through the open windows. Seams of bulging sandstone passed their faces on either side, dark tree roots as thick as a man's arm snaking down; huge ferns, some with flat, bright green leaves which gleamed waxily tropical.

The car rose up again; Mr Taylor slowed it, and unexpectedly swung up a bridlepath. Visible ahead of them seemed to be a rough, empty parking area for the village hall.

'I hope this is right,' said Mr Taylor, doubtfully.

Without a word passing between them, all of the travellers flung open the doors as the engine died, and leapt out. Iz, Chris and Joe groaned, stretched, and jumped about. Perplexed, Mrs Taylor stared at the flapping Ordnance Survey map in her hand and looked further along the track, which continued past the tiny car park and away down into the countryside.

Unexpectedly Mr Taylor said, 'That's it! We're here after all.'

His wife looked to where he was pointing away down the track, which had grass growing in the middle of it in a long stripe.

Chris, not looking, said, 'What? The village hall?'

Iz cantered up to Mr Taylor, Joe following more slowly.

'Whoa! There it is! He's right, you know,' he called to Chris, 'it's the house, there, see?'

'How do you know?' asked Chris dubiously, looking at the distant buildings from beneath his hand to try and cut the dazzle from the sun. They were huddled in a valley all of their own, without a name, a number or, to be honest, a proper street. Iz looked at him as if he wasn't quite right in the head.

'Er, well, it's like, *exactly* the same as the picture of it on the leaflet about the trip they gave us.'

Chris didn't say anything. They hadn't got a leaflet with them to compare it, and how could you possibly remember what the picture looked like? Unlike Iz, he had not unfolded and refolded and gazed at the leaflet for hours and hours over days and days before the trip.

They all stood and stared for a moment as the afternoon sun beat down on them.

Though there was the low grumble of tractors at work somewhere nearby, and a bird sang from a cluster of trees to one side of the path, they were all struck at the same time by a feeling of peace. To the left were soft curves and sweeps of pastureland, two fields of pale sand-coloured arable cutting a gentle contrast. The hedges which bounded them were formed from whole, round-topped bushes; the hedges even turned into small copses and woods in the distance. Flourishing up from the land, wherever the angled corner of one field met another, these looked like great, mossy growths. The high horizon of the hilltops circled them and they could see nothing at all beyond. To the right of the track, the land seemed to do the same, but the sudden grouping of trees to this side slightly obscured their view.

Down ahead of them the track ran towards the house. There was a verge either side, of tall rich grass with flowers waving amongst the blades, but all of this somehow kept itself from sprawling over the edges of the pale, rammed stone track. A simple post and wire fence divided verge from field almost invisibly. The track dipped away from them in the distance, reappeared from between some more trees, and at the end of it, they could just see the house, nestled below one of the highest hills, which flowed up like a green wave behind it.

For some reason everyone just wanted to wander down that track.

Mrs Taylor looked at her husband.

'Shall we come back for the car later?' she said, but Mr Taylor was already nodding even as she asked the question.

He was pleasantly surprised when Chris, Joe and Iz all nodded eagerly. It had been his experience that many of his students often had boundless energy to be wasted within the confines of a dangerous Science Lab, or during a very important Assembly, but were always perversely exhausted when asked to walk anywhere with a purpose.

'Great!' said Iz, and scampered ahead. The others followed at a steadier pace.

Joe took in great lungfuls of air as they strolled along. Flowers and grass and – what was that smell that reminded him of all his country visits?

Mr Taylor had noticed the loud sniffs.

'Cows, Joe? I love that smell. A lot of people don't.'

Chris and Iz wrinkled their noses and made faces of disgust at Mr Taylor and each other.

Iz skipped ahead, and darted suddenly to the left. He stopped at the wire fence, reached down and picked some grass stalks, and stretched over the fence as far as he could reach.

A squat bush and a tall tree obscured the view of the field, but Mr Taylor said, 'I think Iz has found the cows all right.' As they drew nearer, he called out, 'Do mind the barbed wire, Iz.'

Joe hurried to Iz's side, and peered at the black and white cows which hung back from the fence, lowering their heads and rolling their eyes at the boys.

'Not very big,' said Chris dismissively, standing, Joe noticed, at a safe distance on the track with the teachers.

'Heifers,' said Joe.

'What?'

'They're only heifers,' said Joe irritably. 'They wouldn't be very big, would they?'

'Young ladies, Chris,' explained Mrs Taylor, sensing an argument.

Joe turned back to the cows. Chris was supposed to be one of the clever ones, wasn't he? How come he didn't seem to know anything?

'Do you know much about cows then, Joe?' asked Mr Taylor encouragingly.

'Not really,' said Joe, because he didn't know what Mr Taylor meant by 'much', but it probably meant the entire contents of lots of large books. 'My dad just used to work with them, that's all.'

'Oh?' said Mr Taylor, waiting uncertainly. There had been some confusion over whether Joe's father had died, or simply wasn't around, and Mr Taylor couldn't really remember what had been discovered in the end. He just knew that Joe very rarely mentioned him. However, Joe didn't say any more.

So I know stuff that doesn't matter, he thought, and I suppose Chris knows about stuff that does. Graphs and angles and lots of big words in very small print, time zones across the world; and the worst thing is, I don't even know *why* it matters.

*

Back at the head of the track, on the road, Mr Evans had really had enough. The minibus was stuffy in spite of the open windows, and the students, sensing the end of the journey, were becoming fractious and excitable.

Helen, always chatty with her friends, had felt strange amongst a group she didn't know well. When the boys behind and in front of her became too annoying she laid about her with her arms or feet. Miss Ermine would try to interest them in the sights from the windows or obligingly listened to snatches of music on proffered headphones, or admired a mobile phone. But even she was running out of tactics.

Mia, sitting silently as she had done for most of the journey, alongside Miss Ermine, gazed slightly upwards at the sky. Helen, with the rest of the travellers, craned her neck at the windows and tried to see the house.

'Is that it?' someone said.

It nestled amongst the land as if the land must once have waited for it to be placed just there. Slightly obscuring it to the right were trees and a long barn, sloping down with its roof parallel to the falling land.

They crossed a suggestion of a bridge, the trees so thickly clustered below them on either side that they could just see patches of deep black between them, and could not tell if it was water.

Mr Evans pulled up where the track ran into a semi-circular parking area. Beyond this, it continued only as two lines of bricks set into grass, running between the house on one side and the cottages on the other.

The students pushed each other out, but more slowly than they would normally have disembarked, slightly awed by the surroundings. Much as they had looked forward to the trip, one never knew, with school, what it would turn out like. For a start, it was usually raining. Here they were, in what seemed to be one of the most beautiful places in the world, and the sun really was shining and the birds really were singing.

Mr Evans was just starting to say, 'I wonder what's happened to . . .' when Iz, Chris and Joe wandered aimlessly around the corner of the house, followed by Mr and Mrs Taylor.

CHAPTER FIVE

Mia had followed Miss Ermine closely, and now took her arm in a determined manner. She didn't, as a rule, like new things, but was feeling better than she had thought. Still, she liked to keep her safe, familiar person close by in case she was needed.

The group turned to walk round to the front of the house when suddenly Mr Taylor, at the head, came face-to-face with a man approaching. Everyone came to an abrupt halt, Joe cannoning into the back of Chris who turned and scowled.

The man was smiling enquiringly and Mr Taylor scanned him, preparing to explain their presence, trying to make out who he might be. He didn't look like a Professor. He was one of those people of vague middle age, of average height, sturdily built with an outdoor tan and short, golden, thinning hair; plain white cotton shirt, sleeves rolled up revealing sinewy forearms; dull green trousers.

'Hello, we're the party from Briarwood School,' said the teacher.

The man smiled and held out his hand.

'Nice to meet you all,' he said slowly, looking around the

group as Mr Taylor shook his hand. 'I'm David. I'm here to make you all at home. I'll be leading one of the field study groups.'

He spoke slowly, as if there was all the time in the world; and suddenly the urgency to explore, to rush into the house and garden, left the group, and they were in no hurry. He had a nice voice. It was good to stand and listen to it.

'Gwyn will be looking after some of you, too, and Johan –' did his eyes just flicker as he looked at us then? thought Iz, watching the man scanning the youngsters, '– he's come all the way back from Australia, he'll be taking another group under his wing. But you must be tired and thirsty after that long drive. Come on in, come on in,' said David, and turned and led the visitors round the corner of the house to the front.

The group made a little collective noise between 'Ah!' and a sigh as they saw the front of the house. Why, they did not quite know. The house wasn't really grand, or stately; but it wasn't quite like any other house they had seen.

There were white spiked railings springing from in front of it which seemed slightly odd in the middle of the countryside. There were two great stone columns either side of the white wrought-iron gates, with panels carved into them and topped with what looked like stone Eiffel Towers; their dark, warm earthy colour was marbled with some kind of white lichen.

Ancient, cracked flagstone steps led up to the gates. Standing at the foot of the steps, the house towered above the visitors, and they could barely see the grey slate roof.

The house was wide; very wide, thought the children,

staring. Four large sash windows, set into slight arches in the brickwork, stared blankly down at them from above a jutting rail of stone bisecting top and bottom of the house. Below the stone rail, another four massive windows mirrored those above.

Below a white canopy and roof supported on its own carved pillars, a white, immaculately painted front door with a brass knocker stood dead centre.

The short dark turf grew right up to the wall and railings and ran between the broken flagstone steps; little flowering plants sprouted out of the wall and path. All over the brickwork, which glowed soft ember colours of black, orange and red, the soft, white lichen grew.

David stood smiling, waiting at the top of the steps, holding the gates open for them, and the whole party gave itself a little shake and stepped up after him. Helen noticed that the gates contained complicated patterns in the twisted metal, like spider webs.

They followed David politely, carefully, into the house.

A huge, cool entrance hall greeted them, with a dark stone-slabbed floor. The walls were clad with wooden panels; not the dark wood Mr Taylor expected, but painted in bright, beautiful turquoise and picked out at the scalloped edges in gold. Through an open door, they caught glimpses of other rooms and more colours: crushed strawberry, corn yellow, saffron.

They passed through an open door of very old wood, into a vast room with great stone pillars and a huge open fireplace with a complicated carved decoration of twisted rope around it.

'It's like a castle,' gasped Joe to Iz.

Mr Taylor looked around again towards David, and saw that a woman had entered the room. She said nothing, but her incredible beauty seemed to create a natural silence in the group. She had long, dark hair almost to her waist, smooth and shining. Her face had the still, ageless beauty of statues and ancient paintings.

'This is Gwyn,' said David simply to the attentive group. The woman smiled a gentle acknowledgement but said nothing.

'As I said, Gwyn will take one of the study groups tomorrow. She will also be showing that group to their rooms. I'll do the same for my group, as will Johan when he gets here.'

Amid the excitement, Miss Ermine glanced anxiously at Mia, but Mia seemed to remain calm, humming in her funny, high-pitched way while she waited, and stroking her finger round and round the gold detailing of the panelling.

'I'll read out the names of those of you who are going to be with me, then Gwyn's group, and we can get on,' David continued. 'Johan might be here by then, I'm not sure why he's been held up . . .'

Miss Ermine coughed politely. 'I think he's just coming up from the lake, David.'

Lake? thought Mr Taylor, and how on earth does that woman always know these things?

David paused and narrowed his small deep-set eyes at her for a moment.

'Oh, good, thank you Miss – er?'

'Ermine,' she said simply.

'Ah, yes,' said David, and glanced, ever so briefly, at Mia before eyeing the list in his hand.

As he was about to begin reading names, a figure rushed in through the doorway behind him. Lanky, a faded T-shirt with holes in it, jeans hanging off skinny hips, canvas trainers which had seen better days – at first, Mr Taylor took him to be just a boy. But then the face looked up from beneath floppy hair the strange colour of caramel, and he saw serious eyes of a matching shade and realised with a jolt that this was no youth.

'Johan!' said David, relief in his tone. 'At last I can introduce you properly.'

Mrs Taylor looked at the young man with concern. She noticed the unhealthy pallor which hovered beneath the tan, and the urgent looks he shot at David and then the woman called Gwyn, as if he had something desperate to communicate.

If David had noticed, he continued with the introduction nonetheless.

'Johan has been working on a sheep station in Australia for the last year to assist him with his research for his PhD. We had wanted him here – but now, at last, we do have him, and very lucky we are.'

PhD, thought Mr Taylor, surprised. I suppose David has to talk him up because he doesn't exactly impress on first sight.

'Johan is the ecologist; my area is physics; Gwyn is a biologist and chemist; the Professor, who is currently away, is all of those and is also involved in the field of genetics.'

Most of the youngsters goggled slightly at this. Previous

trips involving field studies hadn't been exactly strenuous, academically.

'Johan's group will be . . .' continued David, scanning the list, 'Joseph Turner, Iz Hearn, Mia Sharpe, Helen Blake. If those people would like to make sure they have their belongings and follow him, I'll read out the others.'

The teachers exchanged glances. That lot, put all together, with the least senior leader? At least he would have Miss Ermine to assist.

David was reading out the other names now. Chris was delighted to hear his name called out with Charlie's in the group which was to be Gwyn's.

Helen was pleased to be with Iz. At least she knew him. She hurried over, and he cheerfully led her and Joe towards Miss Ermine and Mia. Johan seemed to be heading in the same direction.

Iz thunked his case down almost on Mia's feet.

'This is great! We got the best bloke, I reckon.'

Johan, arriving at almost the same moment through the throng, must have overheard this, but said rather desperately:

'Miss Ermine? I think I saw you earlier, didn't I? Could you just hang on with everyone here a second while I tell David something? Or actually, no, you could start off upstairs with them and I'll catch you up. You go through here and take the left of the two staircases and then keep left – you end up in one of the wings – and I'll be right after you.'

Miss Ermine looked at him quizzically, but agreed, leading her group away through the doorway he'd indicated and towards the stairs.

As Johan had said, there were two staircases, running up

opposite walls of another vast room and up to a galleried landing, where they disappeared in opposite directions.

As Miss Ermine started up the left staircase, Mia so close alongside that she almost trod on Miss Ermine's feet in spite of the width of the steps, Iz paused.

Joe stopped too, his hand already on the great, thick rope which hung in scooped shapes along the wall, serving as another banister.

'What's up?' he asked warily.

'Nothing,' whispered Iz. 'I just want to know what Johan had to say to David, that's all.'

Instinct and years of practice told Iz that Miss Ermine would check on the party before she turned off on the landing. He was right.

She paused and checked behind her, in time to see Iz put on a spirited show of leaping up after Mia and Helen.

As soon as she turned out of sight around the corner Iz stopped abruptly and turned, nearly cannoning into Joe.

'What the—?' said Joe, grabbing the rope more tightly as it swung out from the wall on its brass keepers.

'Shhh!' said Iz, 'I'll only be a minute. I bet he's got the heebie-jeebies about being given our group, or something.'

Joe stood undecided for a moment, torn between his friend and not wanting to get into trouble. Then he put down his case awkwardly on the stair, and followed Iz at a cautious distance.

Iz was poised on tiptoe just to one side of the doorway through which they'd come.

He caught sight of Joe and made a silent 'shhh' shape with his lips, holding up his forefinger. Then he waved furiously towards the corner behind him as Joe stood in full view of the open doorway.

Joe trotted over to the indicated position. Iz had his ear pressed dramatically against the wall, but Joe, further away, could hear the conversation of the two men quite easily.

'What do you mean you can't get it? You found it all right?' came David's voice with a hint of exasperation.

'Of course it's located – I just can't quite reach it. Perhaps it's not the right time for me to bring it back. Maybe something has to happen before—'

The deeper voice of the older man interrupted.

'Well, that's the first time for over a hundred years. It's extremely worrying that this happens when our visitors are here. No such thing as coincidence. For some reason, that skull has been put out of the way – and I'll bet the Cutters are behind it. I'll try and get in contact with the Professor. The absence of the skull – we don't yet know what impact that may have. We must make sure no one finds out. Johan, you'll have to get it back in time for the end of the tour tomorrow. That Miss Ermine is very capable, I think. You'll have to sneak off and grab it when you see a moment. They won't notice. You'll only be gone a minute.'

Johan sounded doubtful. 'Well, I'll try, it's just, as I said, there was a problem. Still, maybe things will have changed tomorrow . . .'

Just then, there was a tremendous crash, and a series of thuds from the staircase behind the boys.

CHAPTER SIX

The voices stopped suddenly, and Iz and Joe turned around in time to see Mr Evans apparently descending the last steps of the staircase in a series of athletic leaps.

Arms flung out for balance, he flew the last three steps with his outstretched toe just touching one of them, and landed, with a trip and a stagger, on both feet at the bottom.

Iz was so impressed he completely forgot that he and Joe had no business to be where they were.

'Well done sir, wow, I didn't know you could do that! Well, I suppose you're not allowed to, at school . . .'

'What STUPID IDIOT left that case on the stairs?' bellowed the teacher. They could see the colour rushing back to his face, which they now realised had bleached with shock.

'Um . . .' said Joe, frozen in horror at the double trauma of having been caught snooping around and now having almost killed a member of staff.

Joe didn't like shouting. His mum had had boyfriends who shouted. Joe particularly didn't like big men shouting. It made him freeze, which made teachers angrier, because often they were trying to make him move somewhere. It made him unable to speak, which made them angrier still if they were waiting for an explanation or an apology. And when they got angrier, Joe could do only one of two things: run if he could break out of the freeze, or square up to them and shout back if he couldn't. Both responses had got him into very serious trouble.

Iz knew Joe well enough and said rapidly:

'It's me, sir, I left it there. I stopped to come back and give Joe a hand with his.'

Joe unfroze slightly and looked down at his feet. There stood Iz's case, where Iz had placed it before they'd stopped to listen.

Mr Evans gazed speechless at Iz, whether in rage, or astonishment at the idea that Iz might help someone with his bag, Iz couldn't quite judge.

By now, both boys and teacher were aware of David and Johan standing and staring at them in the open doorway.

Johan gave Iz a rather sidelong glance and broke the silence:

'Are you all right, Mr Evans?'

'Yes, yes,' said Mr Evans gruffly, giving himself a brisk sportsmanlike shake and blowing out two deep breaths in quick succession.

'Lucky for you it was a gymnastic member of staff, Iz,' said David, fixing the boys with a stern look from his pale eyes. 'Anyone else might have been badly hurt, or killed.'

Mr Evans loosened up even more at this, and put his hands on his hips and jogged on the spot for a moment, rolling his head around on his neck as if warming up as a substitute about to run in from the benches to save the match. The boys looked at him admiringly.

'Go on, straight upstairs and turn left. You'll find your rooms,' said David, before anyone could say anything else, and moved in to talk to Mr Evans as the boys skipped past him.

'Godalmighty, Iz, why did you want to do that?' hissed Joe.

'To get you out of a freaking mess, of course,' Iz hissed back.

'No, I mean go and listen like that. We could have got in trouble.'

'Not nearly as much trouble as if you had killed Mr Evans, you plonker. What did you want to go leaving your case on the stair for?'

'I'd just lugged it halfway up and it nearly killed me. I wasn't going to drag it all back down just to drag it back up again, was I? God, you're right,' Joe said, suddenly horrified, his tone changing as he stopped at the top of the stairs.

'I know I am, and I keep telling you, you don't have to call me God,' Iz smirked.

'No, but Iz, I could have been done for murder!'

'Don't worry,' said Iz calmly, 'it would only have been manslaughter. You'd have to have *meant* to kill him for it to have been murder.'

Suddenly Miss Ermine was behind them in the corridor leading away from the landing.

'What's all this about murder?' she asked in her soft voice.

'You're not on about that skull, are you?' asked Helen, suddenly appearing beside her and eyeing the boys cynically. 'Because it's not a murder story or anything. It's thousands of years old they reckon, and just got picked up and brought here from something-or-other Pen where we're going on the field studies.'

'Pilsdon Pen,' put in Miss Ermine helpfully, 'I think it's an Iron Age burial mound.'

Iz faltered a moment at the mention of the skull, and felt Joe itching to say something about the conversation they'd overheard. It would be no good giving him a nudge to warn him to shut up, because Joe was one of those people who would say loudly: 'Ow! Why did you just stick your elbow in me, Iz?' However, Joe was someone who needed time to get thoughts and words together, so Iz managed to throw him by launching into a lively and graphic description of Mr Evans' brush with disaster, and avoiding any mention of eavesdropping. From this, Joe realised he wanted to keep their news secret, though he couldn't imagine why. He had a sudden sense of foreboding about Iz's motives.

'Come in and see our rooms, anyway!' said Helen when Iz had finished, and opened a wooden panelled door off the corridor. 'This is just for us girls,' she explained, as the boys peered in and saw a large, sunny room with very old, dark floorboards. Mia was sitting on a bed below the window, engrossed in her favourite book, and Helen's soft toys were spread on another.

'There's a connecting door here,' Helen pointed out, as if she was showing around prospective purchasers. She swept briskly round behind the boys and headed to the open doorway. 'And *your* room is— oh! Hello! I'm sorry.'

Helen was so caught up with her little tour that she had nearly walked straight into Johan, who was standing in the corridor straight outside the door.

'No, no,' said Johan, smiling, 'I was just coming to check you all knew where you were to be staying and so on, but I can see you are managing very well.' And he stood back with a little bow.

Helen, flushing slightly with embarrassment, flicked her hair back and adopted a slightly less confident tone under Johan's gaze.

'Er, well, Iz and Joe, and this is your room, here.'

She opened yet another door in the wall on the right, and the boys rather unceremoniously bundled past her with their cases.

'Yes! Wow! Very nice, eh, Joe?' said Iz, grinning and gazing at the large window which had a view of the fields and the track they'd walked to the house. As in the other rooms, the floor was polished old wood, the carved wooden beds were solid and had big, soft-looking mattresses and pillows, and there was an ancient wardrobe to share between them. They had a bedside table each; the walls and curtains were the pale, buttery yellow of clotted cream.

Joe stood speechless and nodded slowly. He put his case down on the floor but made no move to sit on his bed as Iz was now doing, giving a gentle test bounce. Iz looked at Joe, trying to fathom what he was thinking.

'I'll be back downstairs, if you want anything,' said Johan from the doorway. 'When you've unpacked and so on, come down to that room we gathered you all in, you know the one?'

They nodded.

'Then you can all have something to eat and drink,' he called back as he disappeared.

Iz started to pull things out of his case and push them roughly on to shelves in one side of the wardrobe. His activity didn't seem to have the desired effect of making Joe do the same. Iz stopped unpacking.

'Joe, are you all right, mate?' he asked awkwardly. 'You're not homesick or something, are you? Or would you rather have this bed? Because I don't mind.'

Joe turned away from the window and towards Iz, and suddenly went and sat down heavily on his own bed. Iz noticed that his friend was avoiding his eyes, and looking more closely, realised with shock that Joe was nearly crying.

'Of course I'm not bloody homesick!' Joe blurted out, the anger almost hiding the catch in his voice. 'You've been round mine. Who could be homesick for *that*?'

'Well, you know, I, er, you never know how these things take people . . .' said Iz vaguely. It was very difficult. True, Joe lived in a complete hole, a pit, a dump, though he tried to keep his own room as nice as he could. There was a mad old woman downstairs who was supposed to be Joe's mother, who Joe seemed to ignore and Iz had only spoken to twice. But Iz had never really commented, and now he just didn't know what to say. He could tell Joe was angry, and that anything he was likely to say would be wrong, in the current situation.

'I don't know what's the matter,' said Joe suddenly and unexpectedly, rubbing his eyes with his hands.

'You - you do like it, though?' ventured Iz carefully.

'It's lovely, of course it is. It's just . . .' Joe lifted his head from his rounded, sagging shoulders and looked around the room, not bothering to hide his reddened eyes. 'It's just it makes me feel sort of angry, I don't know why.'

Iz was out of his depth with this sort of talk. He would

have liked a kind Learning Support assistant or someone to take over now. He wondered whether he could get Miss Ermine to come in and see Joe. But he supposed Joe would be cross with him and embarrassed. What would she say at this point? Why do you feel angry, Joe? But he'd just said, hadn't he, he didn't know why?

To Iz's surprise, Joe continued.

'I think it's just that, when you live in a place like mine, you know other people don't, because you go round their houses. And of course I know people live in places like this because you see stuff on telly. But I suppose I almost didn't really believe it. But this is real. Other people really live like this. And they always have done. They probably don't even think it's strange. And it makes me cross, for some reason. Not with them. It's not their fault. I wouldn't want anyone to live where I do. It's just I'm cross for me. Really cross. Cross with whoever's to blame.' And he put his head back down, sniffing loudly and angrily, and furiously wiping his eyes.

Iz sat, uncharacteristically silent. Joe wasn't one for talking – at least, not at length. He didn't think he had ever heard his friend join that many sentences together in one go before, and he had known Joe for ever. He tried to think of it from Joe's point of view. It was tricky. If there was someone to blame, he supposed it would be Joe's mum, or even his dad. But Iz knew that Joe couldn't possibly let himself blame his mum. She wasn't – well. His dad – who knew? And Social Services – well, Joe couldn't really expect them to hand people places like this. Iz decided to give up the problem of blame. He could only help Joe from his own angle.

'You know *I* can't stand it at home, Joe. I'm off out of it as soon as I'm sixteen, I've told you,' he said gently. 'I know it's not like your place, but it's just as bad to be around in a different way. At least you don't get people on in your ear all the time, and trying to ground you, and rows and so on. I know it used to be like that for you too. But at least now you have your own space.' Because she doesn't care about him, thought Iz, no one cares about him. He thought quickly.

'I mean, I know it's probably worse than for me, it's just, I don't get the same feeling as you about this place. I just think it's a great break. For now. I know it's only a week, but I'm not thinking about that. I just feel really – lucky. What with school and everything. I didn't really think it would come off at all.'

He waited for an explosion from Joe. But to his surprise, his friend was smiling at him.

'You're right, Iz. I am such a plonker, aren't I? I'm sorry. Something good comes along and I can't just enjoy it.'

Iz gave a faltering smile back and felt safe to continue:

'And don't forget, I'm leaving home at sixteen. You can move in with me. It won't be like this, of course, but it will be better than we've got now.' He pushed from his mind the worries he had late at night about the where and the how, and with what money. He hoped Joe wouldn't ask those questions just yet.

There was a tap at the door.

'Boy-oys! Are you decent?' Helen opened the door slightly and stuck her head through the gap.

'Come on, we've got to go downstairs – honestly, what have you been doing all this time? You haven't unpacked hardly anything. Oh, Iz, look at that!' Helen was gazing in consternation at the open wardrobe with clothes screwed up roughly on to the shelves. In one stride she was across the room and refolding at the speed of the light before Iz could say a word.

'There!' she said, surveying the neat piles. 'Now the door should actually shut properly.' And she closed it neatly to demonstrate.

'You'll just have to do the rest later before bed.' She looked at Joe's unopened case by his bed but said nothing. She had noticed his slightly puffy eyes.

'How are you about your roommate, Helen?' asked Iz.

'She's all right,' said Helen, 'I like Mia.'

'Oh, yeah, so do I. She's fine. I don't really know her very well,' said Iz rapidly, not wanting to get on Helen's wrong side.

'Now listen,' said Helen moving in between them both and lowering her voice to a stage whisper, 'Miss Ermine wants to sort of, wean her off a bit. You know, stop Mia hanging off her the whole time. She asked me to give her a hand with that. And you two. Try and get Mia to join in a bit more like any normal kid. Mia's mum is having a baby – any day. Mia's going to have to be a bit more grown up.'

'Oh. Oh right,' said Iz, rather doubtfully. 'She seemed pretty grown up to me already. But . . .'

'Yeah, I know what you mean; she is. But she's got used to always having an adult around with her, hasn't she? I mean, she doesn't exactly hang out with the rest of us at break and lunch, does she?'

'Well that's because she doesn't want to,' said Joe sensibly, 'so they let her go to the Learning Support room. I used to, for a bit,' he admitted, embarrassed.

'Well, anyway, I said we'd try and help. You know, make her welcome. Offer to do stuff with her instead of Miss Ermine having to do it all the time,' said Helen.

Iz nudged her sharply. Mia was standing in the doorway, looking at them in her slightly sideways manner.

'Hello, Mia,' said Helen brightly. 'We were just coming. We're all going to go downstairs and get something to eat and drink.'

'Yes,' said Mia firmly, waiting.

For some reason, they all smiled at this. Joe was reminded of his little sister. Mia didn't seem to mind, or think they were laughing at her. The boys stood up and they moved towards the doorway, Mia standing back politely to let them pass. As Joe went past, Mia caught his arm suddenly. He stopped and looked at her.

'What?'

She stared at his face and put up her hand to it, slowly, and gently but firmly pressed her fingers around his eyes. Joe stood patiently, puzzled but unafraid. He looked into the moving-sea eyes but found nothing he understood there.

'Sad,' Mia announced, and to everyone's surprise, held her arms wide. When Joe made no move, she threw them around him and hugged him. It wasn't a soft, comforting sort of hug. Joe felt as if he was being hugged formally, by a man, by a comrade-at-arms at some award ceremony for bravery. He laughed.

'Thank you, Mia. Not sad now.'

Mia released him with no sign of embarrassment and followed him out of the door.

CHAPTER SEVEN

In the general business of sitting down to good food and drink, and listening to an itinerary of their field trips read out afterwards by David ('He seems to do all the talking,' said Mr Evans, leaning over to Mr Taylor, 'I wonder if she ever speaks,' indicating Gwyn with his eyes), there was no time for Iz and Joe to discuss the conversation they'd overheard.

Then, refuelled, the whole group had a quick tour around the outside of the house and gardens and had the geography of the land pointed out to them from the track at the front of the house. There was the lake, twinkling away in the gathering dusk below the house. If one followed the path from behind the house and around behind the hill, it led to Pilsdon Pen.

They discovered that two of the little cottages opposite the house were inhabited by David and Gwyn respectively, with the third left available for a visiting member of staff – at the moment, Johan.

'What are the barns and outhouses for?' asked Mrs Taylor, pushing her rather wild, bushy hair from her eyes and peering around at the barns as if hoping to see inside.

'Oh, a bit of a hobby in our spare time,' said David quickly. 'There's always been a rope and net industry hereabouts. Birdport, nearby, was famous for it. I like to dabble, see how they did it in the old days, repair and so on. Gwyn does a bit of weaving.'

'Birdport was famous for making the hangman's rope,' said Gwyn suddenly. The quietness of her voice had the odd quality of cutting through other noise and hanging alone in the air.

There was a pause for a moment. The faces of the younger listeners turned to her in a mixture of awe and excitement.

Mr Taylor broke the uneasy silence with a little chuckle.

'Well, not a lot of call for that, nowadays.'

'Rope and net has all sorts of uses,' said David reassuringly, looking around the group. 'A rope or a net can save, as well as take, life.'

Mr Taylor interrupted in his teacher voice:

'It seems to have been a long day, somehow. Everyone must be very tired. All of you need to go upstairs now and do any last unpacking, then bathroom and bed.'

Very few cries of distress greeted this announcement, and those were only uttered by a few students out of a sense of duty. In reality, none of them could wait to crawl into those cool, soft-looking beds.

Once in their own room, Joe said to Iz: 'Why didn't you let on to the others about the skull?'

'Because David said it was important that no one knew, of course,' said Iz prissily. 'Honestly, Joe, do you think I'd go blabbing on about it?'

He rummaged through the wardrobe, pulling the folded clothes about, until he found his pyjama shorts.

Joe thought for a moment.

'But David and Johan didn't want *anyone* to know, including us. We shouldn't have been listening, Iz.'

'Well, I wasn't to know that, was I? I wouldn't have been listening if I'd known they hadn't wanted us to. But I couldn't *un*listen, could I? The least we can do is keep it quiet, now we do know.'

Joe always found it difficult to follow Iz's lines of reasoning in cases like this. But he did know his friend well enough to be suspicious. If he wasn't sure why he felt suspicious, it didn't matter. He was usually right. Trouble always followed, in one form or another.

'Aren't you going to open your case?' asked Iz, now pulling his clothes off under the covers of his bed and dropping items one by one into a heap on the floor.

Joe recognised the change of subject as a strategy to divert him, but he turned to the case and began opening it.

Cautiously, he picked through the unfamiliar clothes and wash items bought and packed for him by the school, making little sounds of approval. As he placed them in neat piles in the wardrobe, he said casually: 'Where do you think Johan is going to look for the skull tomorrow? And what on earth was he on about – "can't quite reach it" and "not the right time" and all that?'

Iz pulled himself up on his elbow eagerly.

'I know, I just couldn't follow that at all. And what was that bit about something having to happen before he could – but he didn't seem to know what? Very weird. And David – he reckoned the "Cutters" were behind it. Local family or something?'

While they talked, Joe was getting himself slowly into bed. Hearing adult footsteps along the corridor, he switched off the bedside lamp.

They waited for the sound of retreating footsteps to fade. Then Joe whispered in the darkness:

'Iz?'

'Mmm?'

'Johan's going to try and get the skull tomorrow. When he's out with us. I wonder where it is?'

'I can't think. I thought maybe a tide or something. That's something you have to wait for, for it to change.'

'But we're not that close to the sea. And David said it would only take him a minute. And that when he skived off we wouldn't really notice.'

'I know. And anyway, if it was a tide, Johan would know what had to change and when, for him to reach it. He didn't seem to *know* what was stopping him from getting it. Oh, it's just too weird,' Iz finished up, exasperated.

'Well, at least we can keep a close eye on him and notice when he sneaks off,' said Joe.

'He might need our help. He might even ask.'

'I bet we *could* help. But I don't think he can ask, because David told him not to tell anyone. And he doesn't know we know.'

'Maybe we can just hang about and be in the right place at the right time,' said Iz.

Both boys were content with that. They were very tired. It could wait till morning.

Helen had had a slightly difficult start to the night. Mia hadn't been too keen on the bathroom, for some reason; in fact, refused point blank even to enter it. They had shown her Miss Ermine's and, eventually, this seemed to meet with Mia's approval. Helen walked in and out of both bathrooms with Miss Ermine afterwards, trying to see the difference between them.

'The window's in a different place,' she offered doubtfully.

'Yes, that's true. But I'm not sure that would be it,' said Miss Ermine.

Helen said suddenly, 'Why on earth are we doing this? Why not ask Mia?'

Miss Ermine shrugged and smiled.

'Why not?'

'Seat,' said Mia firmly, already snuggling down in bed.

Helen and Miss Ermine prowled back to the bathrooms.

'Oh!' both said at the same time, meeting in the corridor. 'One's wooden and one's plastic! Of course!'

They were still laughing when Mr Taylor arrived.

But there was yet another interruption to Helen's sleep. She had just dropped off, when she was disturbed by groans from her roommate.

Used to sharing a room with various younger siblings, Helen hauled herself out of bed and put on the lamp on Mia's bedside table. Blearily, she noticed that Mia hadn't just snuggled down, she had really wrapped herself tightly in the duvet. It was a very warm night. Sure enough, beads of sweat were glistening over Mia's forehead. She spoke to her gently, and tried to loosen the duvet, but Mia gripped it tighter.

Helen tapped on Miss Ermine's door.

'Sorry to bother you,' she said.

Somehow, they managed to exchange the duvet for a sheet

from one of the cupboards in Miss Ermine's room, and Mia didn't seem to mind, wrapping herself back in it tightly. Helen slid the sash window open a little and crawled back into her bed.

So much for a rest and a change, she thought, slipping off to sleep.

CHAPTER EIGHT

Joe never found it difficult to wake in the morning – he was used to getting himself up. This morning, he had woken with the light from the sun gleaming through the curtains.

He washed and dressed, not particularly quietly, but it had no effect on his friend, who was lying in his bed as if thrown there, head hanging over one edge, a foot diagonally out over the other.

'Oi! Iz! Wake up!' He looked for something to drive his point home and found one of Iz's trainers.

This was enough to force Iz into shaky action. He staggered to the bathroom, hitting the door frame as he left the room and swearing loudly.

Half an hour later they were all seated around the breakfast table, clearing away the remains of toast, eggs, sausages and bacon, as David, Johan, Gwyn and the staff discussed the itinerary for the day by the huge room's cold fireplace.

'OK, everyone,' announced David, when the last fork had clattered to rest. 'As you know, we start the day with a thorough tour of the place, so you'll know your way around properly. Could you come in your groups to your field study leader, please?'

There was a shuffling of chairs. David, Johan and Gwyn stood separately across the front of the room and waited for their charges; Mr and Mrs Taylor and Mr Evans, looking relaxed and feeling unnecessary, stood to one side.

Miss Ermine waited for the group to head towards Johan before getting to her feet. She hoped Mia would follow them, and for a moment, she did, but then paused and waited. Miss Ermine sighed.

As requested the evening before, the students had brought clipboards and pens and stood ready and eager, Iz flapping his about and testing its strength by hitting Joe firmly on the head. When Joe objected, Iz tested it on his own.

'Stop that, Iz,' said Miss Ermine without heat. 'Concentrate now on what Mr – er . . . ?'

'Semos. But everyone can call me Johan,' smiled their guide.

'Thank you. Concentrate on what Johan has to say, everyone, and follow closely. We don't want to get lost,' said Miss Ermine.

Iz and Joe looked intently at Johan, not so much because of Miss Ermine's instruction, but because they were wondering whether he was thinking about his mission to find the skull. Beneath the boyish smile, he did still look rather tense.

'Thank you, Miss Ermine. Well, first of all, let's tour the other wing. You'll have seen from the outside that the house is like a horseshoe, or a square if you count the back garden wall. Your bedrooms are in one wing, or one side of the horseshoe; the other wing is where there are a few more bedrooms, but downstairs are the labs and so on.'

He spoke lightly and quickly.

Other groups had disappeared by now in different directions; Chris Winter was telling Mr Taylor that he'd forgotten his clipboard and was being told to retrieve it from his bedroom. Without more ado they followed Johan, back into the central room with the staircases leading out of it. This time, instead of taking the stairs, they passed beneath the one on the right and through another huge, wooden door which creaked. Once through, they were in a rather dark corridor.

'It's like a tunnel,' said Joe, stepping carefully.

They peered into laboratories which they seemingly weren't allowed to enter. These weren't entirely dissimilar to their Science labs at school, so no one was too disappointed.

Then they came to a very old, very dark door, with a handle of carved, twisting wood. The same twisting design was carved around the door frame.

'Oh!' said Helen softly. 'How beautiful. I thought it was snakes at first, but it's rope, look, carved out of wood. How clever,' and she stroked her finger around the dusty contours.

'Very old, this part of the house,' said Johan, and opened the door. 'This is the Professor's room, when he's here. We can't go in, but I just thought you'd like to see everything.'

Miss Ermine and Mia hung back; Joe, Iz and Helen crowded into the large doorway. Light spun in through a slightly cobwebby window, which looked away on to the great green hill behind the house. There was a big desk, bookshelves crammed to overflowing, specimen jars. They had no idea what a Professor's room should look like, and though Helen might have expected a little more order, they were satisfied.

They drew back politely as Johan closed the door. Miss Ermine took the lead as they walked further on down the corridor. She seemed to speed up before disappearing around a bend in the panelled walls.

Trying to shake off Mia a bit, thought Helen. 'What do you think so far, Mia? Do you like the house?'

Mia seemed to consider for a moment, her face serious.

'Yes,' she said finally.

Johan, following behind, called a halt for a moment.

'I've just remembered something,' he said. 'I'll just pop back for it. Won't take a second. You go on and catch up Miss Ermine, tell her I'm just coming. You can prowl about a bit from here on – there's nothing out-of-bounds.' He gave a nervous laugh and turned away quickly, walking back the way they'd come.

Iz gave Joe a sideways look. Helen didn't seem to notice. Chattering away to Mia, she walked away up the corridor in the direction Miss Ermine had gone. Iz waited until they were out of sight, and then stealthily headed in the opposite direction, Joe following.

Luckily, the corridor twisted and turned. Iz found that he could sneak along sections, scanning for Johan, without being easily spotted himself. Just as he rounded another bend, he drew back. Joe heard the sharp hiss of Iz's indrawn breath in time to duck back behind him. Iz had spotted Johan disappearing through the door of the Professor's study.

'What is it?' whispered Joe.

'He's gone in the Professor's room. If it's in there, I don't see why he can't just pick it up,' hissed Iz.

'It's not going to be in there, is it? It wouldn't be lost then, would it?' said Joe, practically.

'Well, I don't know. Maybe he's gone to get a key. That's more like it. Let's hang on and follow him when he comes out.'

But he didn't come out. After a few moments, Joe complained.

'We can't just hang around here for ever, Iz. In a minute, Miss Ermine will come along and grab us. Maybe there's another door out of the study.'

'I didn't notice one, did you? But I suppose there must be. Let's just go and have a listen and see if we can hear him rooting around at least,' said Iz, unwilling to release their quarry so soon.

The two boys went across to the door with its carved surround and pressed their ears to it. There was silence.

'He's not in there,' said Iz with certainty, 'there must be another door leading outside. Let's have a look.'

Joe would normally have drawn the line at this, but he was sure, too, that no one could be in such a silent room.

'If he is, we'll just say we were looking for him or something,' added Iz – whether to reassure Joe or himself, he wasn't sure.

Slowly, he pressed the strange, long handle of the door. The carved ropes curved into his palm perfectly. The door swung slowly open without a creak. Inside, the room was exactly as they had last seen it. Johan was not there.

The boys took this in, and then hurried inside. Iz swung the door shut with a gentle click.

'Where's the door he went out of, then?' he said, scouting around. Joe was already pacing, looking. He pulled gently at a bookcase.

'What are you doing?' asked Iz, baffled.

'Just checking it wasn't one of those ones that spins round like you see in films, and you can get through into another room. But it's not,' said his friend, disappointed.

'I suppose there's the window,' said Iz. He regularly slid through windows if a door wasn't available, which was often; his mother locked all the doors at home when she wasn't there to stop him getting in if he was playing truant, or even when he wasn't. She didn't trust him in there without her.

But the window had an unused look about it; he noticed the unbroken cobweb across the sliding mechanism and felt pleased at his detective work.

At that moment, the door opened. They froze.

'Johan? Iz? Joe?' came a small voice.

Then Helen's anxious head and shoulders appeared through the gap. One glance showed her that the two boys, looking furtive, were there alone.

'What the— what are you *doing?*' she hissed. 'Where's Johan?'

'Shh!' said Iz. 'We don't know. Get in here quick before someone sees you.'

'We're not really allowed,' said Helen doubtfully, but she hurried in, pulling Mia after her, and closed the door.

'Well?' she demanded.

'We followed him in here all right, but he just isn't here,' said Iz.

'What do you mean?'

Suddenly, Iz took in Mia's presence for the first time.

'Where the heck is Miss Ermine? She's not coming this way?'

'I don't know where she is. It's the weirdest thing. We followed her round the corner, and she just wasn't there. But . . .' She looked sideways at Mia and then back at Iz, and suddenly adopted an unnaturally cheerful tone, 'I think she's probably just popped off to get something and will be back in a moment. Nothing to worry about.'

Iz glanced nervously at Mia. She didn't look worried. She was staring around the room in an interested way. Humming gently, she headed to some tall yellow flowers in a vase on the desk and started to investigate them closely. Joe stopped fiddling with the bookcase and wandered over to her.

'Lovely, aren't they, Mia?' he said. 'Flags, my mum used to call them.'

'Lovely,' repeated Mia, then, as she stroked the leaves and the petals, staring closely at every part, 'three. Three Three Three . . .'

Iz tore his eyes from her and looked back at Helen.

'I suppose we'd better get out of here,' he said.

'Why were you following Johan, anyway?' she asked, looking more relaxed and beginning to prowl around the room.

'We overheard him. Him and David on the first day. They've lost the skull. Johan was saying he knew where it was but hadn't been able to get it. David told him to sneak off and get it back. We thought we might be able to help or something. So we knew he was on to something when he said he'd just slip off for a moment.'

'Hmm,' said Helen thoughtfully. She paused by a mug on the desk.

'How long ago was it since the Professor was here, I wonder? Ugh,' she said, picking up the mug and displaying the contents to Iz, 'mouldy. I won't chuck it on you this once, it'd make a mess.'

'Thanks,' said Iz, backing away.

'Here's something for you, Iz,' said Joe, pointing. There was a calendar, propped near the flowers. Iz came to his side to look. The photograph illustrating that month was of a large, black panther.

'Beautiful! Wouldn't that be something, if we really did see one down here?' said Iz, picking it up to admire it.

There was a rattle of something falling on the floor.

'Careful, Iz, you've knocked over his little stone collection by the looks of it,' grumbled Joe, picking up two little cube-shaped pebbles and putting them back near the calendar which Iz had replaced.

'Ugh!' said Helen again. She was standing near the fireplace, looking doubtfully at a glass case on the mantelpiece. The boys took a glance at the contents of the case and hurried across.

'Wow. It's a crocodile. Only small, but still . . .' said Iz. 'Why did you say "ugh"?' he asked Helen. 'You're as bad as that girl Trudi. Can't stand anything. Breaks a nail and she faints. Never in Biology because everything makes her sick.'

He dodged a blow from Helen's open hand.

'I am NOT like Trudi. I said "Ugh" because I hate stuffed animals, plonker. Especially *baby* stuffed animals. It's cruel. It's sick.'

'Be fair, Helen,' said Joe seriously. 'This is a Professor's room and everything. I mean, look, there's loads of jars of stuff.'

He waved his hand at the shelves of the bookcase. Helen saw that there were bottles and jars with all kinds of bleached, blobby-looking things floating in liquid.

'Most of that stuff seems to be anemones, squid sort of things,' Joe continued, mistaking her expression for one of fascination, then added: 'The croc could have died naturally, anyway. My dad knew someone who stuffed things, and most of them were things he found dead by the road, as long as they weren't too mangled.'

Helen's face, if anything, registered even more distaste at this information. Iz started giggling.

'Yeah, Helen, the croc croaked,' he choked.

Before anyone could react, the door suddenly opened again. They looked around in shock.

Chris Winter stood in the doorway.

'God, it's all of you. I saw Iz and Joe disappearing into here ages ago. You don't know where my lot are, do you? I had to go back and get my clipboard thing, and now I can't find them. You're the only ones I've seen. Where's your bloke then?'

'Um,' said Iz.

'He went off somewhere for a minute,' said Helen quickly, 'I expect he'll be back soon.'

'Oh, I'll come in and wait with you, then, and maybe he can tell me where my group is,' said Chris easily, and stepped into the room and shut the door.

There was suddenly a dull boom, like the sound of a low-flying aircraft; the room went dark for a moment. The walls seemed to shake, and Helen instinctively grabbed on to the nearest arm, which was Iz's, sure that they were in an earthquake. In the darkness, she could see very little, but she felt his warm skin beneath her fingers and clung to it as the only certainty. Joe flung his arm around Mia's shoulders and pressed her safe to his chest; a plane was crashing, but where, on the house, or on the hill behind? Surely the hill? Maybe it couldn't make the height? Chris staggered two steps towards them and grabbed a handful of Iz's T-shirt, twisting it around in his fist to keep himself steady. The walls seemed to vibrate so much, they actually began to blur in front of their eyes. There was a high-pitched whining as the floor shook beneath their feet. *This was it.* Simultaneously, except for Mia, who was crushed into Joe's chest, they screwed their eyes shut and put their heads down, waiting for the explosion, the falling masonry and beams upon their heads.

There was an almighty jolt which took them off their feet; then all was still. Confused, now in darkness, they were instantly aware that their knees and hands were in contact with damp, soft ground; grass, even. They felt around, blind, trying to understand how, whatever catastrophe had happened, it could have blown away the floor from beneath them.

And even then, how could there be *grass?* thought Iz. The high-pitched whining had stopped. He could hear Joe saying, 'I'm sorry Mia. Mia, I'm sorry. Are you all right?' He sounded as if he were nearly crying.

Iz blinked a few times. Screwing up his eyes so tightly had

made them blurry. He looked at the ground in front of his face, and realised he could see. It was dark, like at night, but when the moon is out. He could see his hands, grass. When he looked up, something still seemed to be wrong with his eyes, though. He saw Joe kneeling up and brushing at Mia, who was pushing his hands away determinedly; but beyond them, all was still a blur and darkness.

'Iz! Iz, are you all right?'

He turned and focused on Helen's face: clear, with huge cornflower blue eyes and perfect, English rose skin. He gazed at it wonderingly, and then at the golden halo of her hair. She was real. He could see her. He suddenly became aware of a terrible pain in his forearm.

'I'm all right, except, ow, my arm,' he answered.

Both of them stared at his arm simultaneously and saw Helen's hand, gripping tightly.

'Oh, I'm sorry!' said Helen, realising and snatching her hand away. White and red marks remained where her hand had been.

'God, you stuck your nails in, you witch,' said Iz, rubbing furiously at the marks with his other hand.

'I said sorry. What's the matter with the walls?' said Helen, still crouching, still terrified.

'What walls?' said Iz. 'We're outside. Do you mean that blurriness? I thought it was my eyes.' He called across to Joe.

'Joe, you all right, mate? Stop flapping at Mia like that. Is she all right?'

'I'm fine. I just thought I'd crushed her when we fell over. I think she's OK . . .'

Helen seemed to pull herself together at the mention of

Mia. She crawled forward to where the other girl was kneeling.

'All right, Mia? It's all right, now. Just an accident.'

Iz could tell by her voice that she was trying not to cry. He knew she was trying to be brave to reassure Mia. The girl who couldn't even cope with ordinary stuff like loud noises wasn't likely to cope well with this, he thought.

He looked across at Mia. He found it best to focus on the others. Staring at the blur beyond and around them made him feel rather sick. To his surprise, Mia was the first to get to her feet, brushing herself off, picking off little pieces of grass in a calm, unruffled way.

It seemed to calm Joe and Helen down. Joe wiped his eyes and stood up, and so did Helen. Iz felt something let go of his T-shirt; until then, he hadn't been aware that it had been snagged.

'Christ, Iz,' said Chris's shaky voice behind him. 'Whatever you pulled this time, I think you've really gone and done it.'

Iz turned around, still on his knees. Chris faced him on all fours, looking very white and very sick. Behind him, Iz noticed, the blur remained.

'Don't be a complete plonker. Even I couldn't have done this.'

Iz got slowly to his feet, and Chris, feeling his legs carefully to check they would hold him up, did the same.

'What the hell was that?' said Chris. He rubbed his face with his hands as if to check it was still there, and succeeded in smudging his skin with earth and grass stains. 'God, I wonder if it was an atomic bomb or something. If it was, we've still had it from the radiation.'

'That blur,' said Helen suddenly, 'we aren't in the eye of a tornado or something, are we?'

They looked around and considered, except for Mia, who looked at her feet, apparently unconcerned. It was a comforting theory, one that would make sense. They had seen films. But the way the blur simply existed, did not seem to whirl or turn, and the lack of any sound of wind, meant that they could not believe it, however much they wanted to.

'What happens if we walk into it?' said Iz curiously.

'No, don't, Iz,' said Helen, worried.

'Well, it would be pretty silly not to try. What if we could just step through it and walk back to the house?' he reasoned.

None of them liked to acknowledge that they were out of the house, because they did not see how they could be. They stood and watched Iz walk towards the blur. He held his hand out before he reached it, but his hand simply bounced back gently.

He took a step; his foot rebounded. He could not step through.

'Ah,' he said. He turned and looked at them apologetically. For some reason, he did feel responsible. It had, after all, been his idea to go into the study.

Suddenly, he noticed that the encircling blur was stretching away, growing fainter behind his friends, allowing them more room. As it moved, it revealed the edge of some stonework slightly to the right; some branches, trees. This looked familiar.

'Look!' he shouted, pointing behind them.

The others jumped, startled. Iz had forgotten how afraid everyone still was. Then they saw what he was pointing at.

'It's the brook, and the bridge,' said Joe eagerly. 'We walked over it to the house. Thank God, we know where we are.'

Then all of them saw a movement.

'There's someone down in the brook,' said Helen, starting forward.

They hurried to the edge. As in the bright sunlight of the day, the brook was black as a bottomless hole; for some reason, they could not see the sparkle of water. But they did just catch sight of a pair of hands and caramel-coloured hair as someone lowered themselves down.

'Johan!' shouted Iz, 'It's Johan! Johan, come back you . . .'

He hurled curses down into the darkness. Helen grabbed his shirt.

'Stop it, Iz! Stop shouting! Leave him. He can get the mouldy old skull. We know where we are now. It's just fog. We can walk back to the house.'

Joe and Chris looked at her mutely. They didn't want to remind her that Iz had been unable to pass through what she called fog. Mia looked down into the blackness, the only one of them apparently unfazed.

Iz tore Helen's hands from his shirt.

'You try walking through it. I'm going after him. It's his fault. He got us into this – he must know how to get out.'

Before anyone could say anything else, Iz was sliding down into the brook on his backside, not even bothering to lower himself carefully. A moment later, and he was gone.

CHAPTER NINE

'Iz!' shouted Helen, on the edge of the darkness.

Standing just behind her, Chris swore. All of them gathered round and stared down into the brook.

'Why can't you see down there?' complained Helen. 'You'd think there was water. But you can't actually see it.'

'I didn't hear a splash,' said Joe.

Helen shouted again. There was no reply, no sound of any kind.

Joe started to sit down on the edge and hang his feet over.

'What are you doing?' shrieked Helen. 'Don't even *think* about it, Joe. He could be lying down there in pieces. There's no point in more of us doing the same thing.'

'I'm sure he's OK,' said Joe firmly, 'and anyway, he followed Johan. Johan must know the way.'

'If he was all right, he'd have shouted back up. Why doesn't he answer?' Helen said desperately.

'I don't know,' said Joe. Despite the trouble Iz always led him into, Joe instinctively felt he would be better off in a dangerous situation with his friend rather than this directionless bunch.

Helen saw that his mind was made up.

'If only we had a rope,' she said forlornly, then turned to Chris. She didn't really know him, didn't know what she would make of his judgement.

'What do you think is the best idea, then?'

'Well, I wouldn't go jumping down a black hole just because someone else did,' Chris replied. 'Not till they told me it was OK. Personally speaking, I think the best idea is just to wait here and someone will find us.'

This seemed a sensible idea to Helen, so she didn't know why she felt it was flawed. Perhaps because none of this seemed possible. You waited for help after a building fell on you – but what was this? How were they out here? Why did it seem to be night?

Joe was starting to lower himself over the bank.

'I tell you what, Joe – Joe, listen to me,' said Helen rapidly, crouching near him.

Joe gave an impatient grunt.

'Call to us all the way. As you go down. See if you can call to us from the bottom. Just try, would you?'

'OK,' said Joe. He was concentrating now, as he wasn't very good at physical stuff. He held on for as long as he could feel the earth of the bank with his hands behind him, then shuffled downwards on his backside.

'Going, going . . .' he called back. He looked down. Still only blackness.

With the next shuffle he felt the bank abruptly snatched away from him. His hands floundered, felt nothing. He was falling, falling into complete darkness. The shock sucked the breath out of his lungs and his throat clamped tight with

71

horror. The 'gone' he'd meant to shout out simply rang in his own head.

Then his feet hit something soft, his legs buckled, and he found he was landing, bouncing, landing again, more gently, and finally he lay cradled in – what was that familiar feeling?

Joe realised that he had screwed his eyes tightly shut in terror and had forgotten to open them. Now finding he was not dashed to pieces but was, in fact, lying rather comfortably, he felt brave enough to look around.

He saw some kind of rope netting stretching away all around him. A hammock! That's what the feeling reminded him of. He was lying in a very, very large hammock. There was a gentle, old-gold glow of light replacing the terrible inky darkness. He sat up cautiously. Well, this wasn't exactly a hammock. It was the sort of net you might see under a trapeze artist or something, he realised. He seemed to be in some kind of cave. He called gently, 'Iz! Iz!' but there was no reply. Then he remembered the others, waiting up above. He started to call, 'Hey, Helen!' but as he looked upwards, he could no longer see the hole through which he must have fallen into the cave. There seemed to be just solid, sandy rock above him.

'Oh,' he said quietly. He thought for a moment. Perhaps that's why Iz didn't call up, he thought. Perhaps they can still hear though, somehow, if you do. Feeling rather foolish, he called up to the rock roof, 'Helen? Mia? Chris? It's OK. It's safe. I'm all right.'

Though he didn't shout loudly, he heard his voice rebound around and around. When the echoes died away, he listened carefully. He heard no answer, no sounds from the others.

He set himself on all fours and began to crawl over to the edge of the net. This was harder than he had thought; the toes of his trainers kept jamming through the mesh and he had to stop to free them. The springy tension of the rope meant that every time he grabbed a handhold to move forward, the whole thing shook and swayed and the muscles in his arms started to shake from the effort of keeping himself steady. Finally, however, he made it to the edge, with sore knees where the rope had bitten. It wasn't a very big drop to the sandy cave floor. Gripping with both hands, he turned himself so that his legs could drop over the edge.

Helen and Chris stood looking into the blackness, aghast. They had heard Joe's jokey, 'Going, going,' and had then seen him suddenly swallowed by the blackness, with no further sound.

As they tried to think, to rationalise what they had seen, Mia was taking up a sitting position at the point Joe had pushed off into the dark.

'Mia! What the . . . ? No, Mia, don't. Bad. Dangerous,' said Helen, trying to pull the other girl up by one arm. Chris rushed to grab her other arm, but Mia waved it out of reach. She twisted around and pointed behind them.

Helen stopped and looked.

'Chris. The blur. Isn't it – getting closer?'

Even as she spoke, more of the ground behind them disappeared into a smudged suggestion. Chris turned and looked ahead of them. The tree branches and the corner of the bridge were disappearing too.

'It's not moving forwards,' said Chris, 'it's just closing in on us.'

As they stood staring, distracted, Mia gave a little shove and disappeared. Helen jumped at the slight movement and looked down at where Mia had been.

'I don't believe it,' she said.

Chris was looking at the blur as it narrowed around them, around the edge of the black brook.

'When Iz tried to walk through it, he just sort of bounced off,' he said, looking worried. 'I wonder what happens when it contacts with us . . . ?'

At that moment, the hazy edge of the blur cannoned into him. He felt himself bounce off it, crash into Helen, and then hit another wall of blur which must have closed in behind them.

Helen staggered backwards from Chris, ricocheted off the wall behind her and scrabbled for a footing. She looked down and realised that she was on the edge of the brook. Now there was nowhere else to stand. Chris staggered backwards again; he felt nothing beneath his feet; he grabbed for Helen but missed; then both of them were falling.

Joe, standing on the cave floor and looking around him, could see there was only one rough archway leading out. He had just taken a step towards it when he heard the creak of ropes from behind him.

'Mia!'

He was delighted, for some reason. He didn't want to be on his own down here.

Mia sat up and looked around. Then she tried to crawl over the netting, as Joe had done, to the edge. But Joe soon saw that she was finding it too difficult. He walked over to the edge, wanting to help, but not quite sure how. He called out.

'Mia. Hold the ropes. Hold them as you move your hands . . .'

She didn't seem to take any notice, struggling open-palmed so that her hands shot through the holes of the net, trapping her around each shoulder, her face in the ropes. She floundered out of the grip again somehow and knelt up, catching her breath.

'When you try again, Mia, grab the rope tight . . .'

Mia interrupted him. 'My hands,' she announced formally in her strange accent, 'don't do – what I ask.'

'Oh,' said Joe, taken aback. He'd rarely heard Mia speak, let alone like this. Then he thought about what she'd said. Well, she did have a problem then.

She needed to crawl across a firm surface. If only . . .

'Hold on, Mia,' said Joe, inspired.

He stooped under the net and, reaching Mia, he crouched down beneath her, turning his back to her.

'Can you try using my back to crawl over?'

Mia didn't answer but started to climb over the net where it was taut over Joe's back. Joe gasped as she thumped him firmly with first a flat palm and then a knee. Her second knee was just hitting him in the head when he shouted for her to wait and go slower. In this strange fashion they reached the edge of the net, where Mia grabbed a chunk of Joe's hair as a sort of handle on her way to the floor.

'Owwch!' shouted Joe. 'You might be more careful, Mia.'

Just as he glared at her, dusting herself off, he was aware of the squeak of ropes again. Both turned to see Chris and

Helen flying back up in the air again, before falling back into the net in a tangle of arms and legs.

When Helen had been calmed from a burst of near-hysterics, which seemed to have been caused equally by the shock of the fall to near-certain death and the unplanned physical contact with Chris, whom Helen seemed to believe was to blame, the two managed to crawl over the net and drop from the other side.

'Did you hear me call up, then?' asked Joe.

'No we flipping didn't. We weren't planning to follow you. We just ended up with no choice,' said Helen crossly. 'Mia went after you. We couldn't stop her.'

'What do you mean, no choice?'

'I mean the blur thing kind of closed in on us. Finally we just got shoved down the hole.'

'Oh well. We're down here now. I don't suppose it can get you here,' said Joe.

Chris looked at him doubtfully. He didn't know what rules Joe was applying to the blur, but he had surely noticed that rules were out the window here. There was no hole in the rock ceiling, for a start, to explain how they came to end up in the net. But he decided not to point that out. He'd had enough of Helen's hysterics. Maybe Joe was cleverer than he looked.

'Yeah, that's right,' said Chris. 'We'll just go along a few tunnels and probably find our way out in no time.'

They walked beneath the rock arch and into a large tunnel which glowed softly with a light at the other end. The light became more intense as they walked towards it.

'This must lead outside then,' Chris called back.

But as they neared the glow, they realised that it came

from another, larger cave. In the middle of the floor sat Iz and Johan, Johan looking sunk in the depths of despair with his head in his hands, and Iz looking cross.

When the cries of greeting and brief spats of argument about Iz's behaviour had died down, Chris, Joe and Helen looked round at Johan, who had barely looked up at their arrival.

'What's the matter with him?' asked Helen in her loud hiss, hope plummeting as she looked at the person she had been relying on to get them out of here.

'I don't really know,' said Iz. 'I haven't been here very long. You must have come after me pretty sharpish.'

'No,' said Helen firmly, 'we had a discussion. Then Joe went after you, then Mia but we tried to stop her. Then me and Chris got shoved by the blur, like I said. We must have been – oh, I don't know, what do you think, Chris? How long was it between Iz going and us?'

'I dunno. About ten minutes?'

'Well how come I've just bounced down in that net, walked straight out of that cave and into this one and found Johan just leaving, and then you practically walk straight in?' asked Iz, exasperated.

'Time is different here,' said Johan from the floor. He looked tired. They sensed he'd only spoken to stop an argument.

'What do you mean, different? Where's here?' asked Chris, looking at him narrowly.

'You can't rely on it. Time. It operates differently to the way that you think. You don't arrange events around it. Events arrange time to suit themselves.'

Johan spoke in a dull, matter-of-fact tone. Chris goggled at him. 'Oh. Right. Of course. When we get out of here, I hope you can explain that to the people who will have been out looking for us for hours.'

Chris consulted his watch, trying to remember when they had started all this. That's it, they were touring the house. He walked into that room – it must have been about eight thirty – but his watch seemed to be saying four thirty. It was an analogue watch. Chris tried to work out whether it was four thirty in the afternoon, or the morning. Not the morning – that didn't make sense. And yet neither did the afternoon. And why had it been dark, outside?

Johan looked at the confused young man with sympathy.

'Don't even go there, man. Put away the watch and forget it. And when you get out of here – if you get out of here – no one will have missed you. There will be an extra hour that day, or something.'

'How – *how* could there be an extra hour? What are you talking about? Even if it's that Putting Back the Clocks Day or whatever, people would notice if we weren't there,' Helen burst out impatiently, her voice squeaking off the register.

'People don't pay attention to things,' Johan said vaguely. 'They go by the watches and the clocks. It seems like you've been gone an hour, but they check the time and believe it. They decide their own senses are at fault. It's easy to even stick in extra days, extra weeks. There's often an extra day in the week.'

The youngsters stared at him as if he were mad, except for Joe, who was looking thoughtful and stroking his chin.

'Is it usually a Wednesday?' he asked unexpectedly.

'Yes,' said Johan, 'though sometimes Tuesday seems to do as well. It's not the same everywhere of course. Just groups of interacting people. Maybe an office, maybe a whole village.'

Iz, Helen and Chris now had to turn their heads this way and that, in order to goggle at both speakers. Mia simply looked interested. Joe ignored his friends' looks and continued: 'If that can happen with Time, can it happen with anything you measure?'

'What do you mean?' asked Johan cautiously.

'Well, I've always thought that as well as extra Wednesdays – only in school weeks, I think, never when it's the holidays – the stairs at school seem to get longer in the afternoon. Or higher. Or both. But then I thought, if you measured them in the morning and in the afternoon, the tape measure would read the same amount. But if the measures are all *wrong* . . .'

'Ah! You're right, I think. That's currently still an issue of heated debate. Clever boy though, you're on the side of the leading thinkers, the cutting-edge camp.'

Joe smiled. It felt good knowing you were right. And no one had ever called him clever, not in his whole life. Except sarcastically, when he dropped something or knocked into someone.

The others gazed at him in astonishment.

'Well, I'm glad at least one of us understands it,' Iz said. 'But I, for one, would like to get out of here. And I was just pointing this out to Johan here, who seemed to go all . . .' Iz seemed lost for the right word, and waved his arm around in an elaborately floppy way to illustrate what he meant – '*sad* like this – as soon as he clapped eyes on me.'

They turned and looked at Johan, still sitting on the floor. He had put his head back into his hands, and was grasping at his hair.

He felt their silence and looked up.

'Look, I'm sorry,' he said, not sounding at all sorry, 'I didn't ask to get stuck with you lot down here. You are all just thinking of your bad luck, and wanting to get out. But me – now I know why they wanted me back. It's always another task, another favour. This isn't an accident. I'm stuck down here because of you, as much as you think you're stuck down here because of me.'

CHAPTER TEN

Iz stared down at Johan in disbelief. He'd been blamed for some things in his time, but this really took the biscuit.

'What do you mean, you're stuck down here because of us? Of all the flipping cheek—' began Iz.

'Hang on a minute, Iz,' said Joe suddenly. Iz was surprised at the interruption. He looked at his friend and saw that he was giving him a reproving look. Perplexed, he realised that the others were too. Even Mia.

'What? *What?* Why are you looking at me like that? I couldn't have made all this happen. I just went into the Professor's study looking for Johan. What's so wrong with that? Anyway, nothing happened then. And nothing happened for a while; you –' he pointed at Helen, 'you and Mia came in and still nothing happened.'

Realisation dawned on Iz's face. His pointing finger veered round to Chris.

'It was *you!*'

'What?'

'It was when *you* came in. Everything was fine until then. You just waltzed on in and suddenly, *Boom . . .*'

Iz was shouting now. Chris shouted over him, exasperated.

'But you told me you were waiting for Johan. I thought he'd put you there to wait. I didn't know you'd sneaked in there without permisson. I didn't do anything wrong. For chrissake, I hadn't even started the tour. I just had to go back for my clipboard and couldn't find my group. I didn't even have time to touch anything. I just walked in!'

The two boys were glaring at each other. Helen thought it was time to intervene.

'Be fair, Iz. He didn't know anything about Johan sneaking off to look for the skull. You only knew that because you'd listened in on a private conversation. It could have all happened because we fiddled with something – we did look around the room.'

Iz looked so angry that Helen recoiled slightly.

Chris was asking, puzzled: 'What do you mean, sneaking off, looking for the skull?' but no one took any notice. Joe butted in quickly.

'I don't know why we're all going on about whose fault it was. Johan is the one who should be explaining.'

This calm piece of common sense had the effect of making everyone take a breath for a moment. Iz, still angry, muttered:

'Yeah, well, if we can believe anything *he* says.'

They looked at Johan, still sitting on the floor of the cave. Helen tactfully sat down next to him. Slowly, the others followed suit. There was a moment's pause.

'Where's the light coming from down here, anyway?' asked Joe, to break the ice, and because he really wanted to know. It had been a disappointment when they'd realised the light didn't signify the outside, but he was very grateful for it nonetheless. It had been such a relief to open his eyes after the pitch black of the fall through the brook. Joe hated the dark.

'I think it's crystals in the ceiling. Or maybe some kind of lichen which gives out a glow. I've never investigated it. It does the job though, that's the main thing, isn't it?' answered Johan, sounding relieved that someone, at least, didn't seem to be cross with him.

'You don't know though,' checked Helen, carefully. 'You've been down here before, right? You know where we are? Where to go?'

'Yes, I've been here before. I was here the other day trying to get the skull. I couldn't get to it. I should have known then . . .' and he shook his head, looking depressed again. Chris recognised the need to keep him talking.

'No one's explained to me about the skull business. What's happened, Johan?'

'It disappeared from its place. You were supposed to see it at the end of your tour. It's usually just kept in a drawer in the Professor's room. But we put it out on a little table in one of the corridors, just this once. David asked me to find it, get it back.'

'You said you knew where it was,' said Iz, 'but you couldn't get it. Where is it then?'

'I don't know exactly. It's just here, somewhere, in the Professor's dimension—'

'In his dimension?' interrupted Chris. 'How do you mean? I've heard of dimensions but I didn't know you could get a Professor's Dimension. Is it some kind of experiment?'

Johan sighed. He rubbed his forehead. Helen noticed the strange whiteness which glowed through his skin beneath the tan. It was familiar to her, somehow. She frowned.

'No, it's not an experiment,' Johan said. 'I don't know how much to explain. It would take a long time and is very complicated.'

Joe looked nervous. Everyone else readied themselves and nodded at Johan.

'Go on, then, try us,' said Chris encouragingly.

'Everyone has a dimension,' Johan said. 'A dimension is your reality. You create it. You inhabit it. Dimensions cross, meet. Of course, there are other dimensions too, not just people's.'

Confused, Joe looked around. 'So this isn't real?' he asked. 'It seems real. But then, some parts don't. Like the blur, and the brook.'

'Of course it's real. Real's different for everyone. It's just, for some reason, you are in someone else's dimension.'

'Ah,' they all said.

Mia said it just a fraction after everyone else. Joe looked at her. She just said that because we did, he thought. I don't think she has the faintest idea what he's on about either.

'This is a very special dimension, of course,' said Johan. 'It's been engineered, and you have been engineered into coming here, and so have I. For some reason.'

'Do you mean this has been set up? For us? If this is the Professor's dimension, he must have caused all this,' said Helen crossly.

Johan sighed.

'I'd better start by explaining about nets.'

They looked at him quizzically.

'Not nets like you think – nets go back longer than that.

When a foetus starts growing, cells divide, don't they, and divide again? Instead of a line, things always – branch out, divide, like a rope: spiral, divide, increase, joined and linked all the time. Chromosomes, nerves, the lymphatic system, the circulation, it goes on and on. The same happens everywhere you look. The family tree. Real trees. Eco-systems. Evolution. Communications – not just electronic.' He stopped abruptly, as if tired with the effort of explaining. His voice dropped. 'And events. Events do it too. History. Present. Future.'

He paused for a moment, then, seemingly encouraged by their attentive silence, continued.

'Now, try looking at it another way. David and Gwyn are net-fixers – a very rare breed. The net makes predictable patterns – rather like the weather. Try to imagine the Professor as – as, well, a sort of weather forecaster. You probably all know how that works. Satellites send information, then the forecasters look at the patterns, what's happening all over the world, and try to predict what will happen, maybe in their region.

'The Professor is one of those, mostly – I mean, a forecaster – but of events and outcomes. They too make a pattern. We call it a net.'

Chris said, 'This sounds like crystal ball rubbish to me, but – assuming it *is* scientifically based – are you saying that David and Gwyn make world events take place? That's just . . .'

Johan shook his head.

'No, net-*fixers* not net-*makers*. No one makes the net – that just *is*. David and Gwyn are just two of many, all over the world, who fix the net when necessary so it runs the way we believe it was meant to. That's tricky to figure, of course, so there's actually very little intervention. They are only needed because of the Cutters.'

Iz sat forward, interested.

'The Cutters,' he said, 'they – they stop things going the way that they should?'

'Cutters don't fix anything, they don't make anything – except holes.' Johan's voice was low. He almost spat the words. 'The Professor, you see, has seen a bit of net forming, but it's being hacked at, cut about. David and Gwyn take a look – it's a bit vague, but they try their best – and between them they work out that the net seemed to re-form well if people from your school could be placed at the house in a certain period of time. Now, the net will naturally always try to form; you just have to give it the right ingredients – for the rope, if you like – and it will go on the way it wants to go. The Professor, David and Gwyn have no idea why it's people from your school, why at the house, and who those people will be. The net seems to choose what or who it needs.

'Meanwhile, the Professor never gave a thought to a minor roofing job. He infuriates a temperamental builder when he signs some bit of paper accepting a quote from a rival firm. The skull was, unusually, out on the table for a bit of a dust before your arrival (we always put it out for visitors) – and it must have just occurred to the man, as he left in a huff, to snatch it up . . . The Cutters set it up to happen the way it did.'

'And if a builder chucked the skull – I mean, is he a Cutter?' put in Joe, trying to keep up.

'No, he's just the type of bloke who would do that, given

the right situation; just what the Cutters wanted, without him knowing anything about all this.

'That made us sure that something was supposed to happen on your visit that needed the skull in place. Without it, the pattern of the net started to show a hole in the wrong place.'

They all sat and digested this for a moment.

'Then we need to get the skull back in place.' To their surprise, it was Mia who spoke, calmly and confidently. She gazed back at them and added, 'Then everything will be correct. It is important to have everything right.'

Helen thought, we were all here forgetting Mia and maybe thinking she wouldn't have a clue. But she gets it all right. She sounds so sure. Why do I always have to worry?

'It – it is a good thing that's supposed to happen?' she asked nervously, dragging her eyes from Mia to Johan.

'Well, for the best, as they say, yes,' said Johan, returning to his normal vagueness. 'Otherwise, something will surely go awry.'

'I don't understand why we're in this dimension, though, and why the Professor made it,' said Joe, his brow furrowing.

'The Professor can't *make* it exist – dimensions just *do* exist. But he can adapt it. He leaves open the channel to his reality as a safety rope – when there's a cut to the main rope of the net, as there has been, this little string hangs, left behind, still joining the net as it was meant to be. People like me can use it to find out what's going on, to effect a repair on David and Gwyn's advice. It allows time, when there is none. There are many similar connecting threads. They can be incredibly dangerous, delicate and thin as they are, and taking such a lot on themselves. The net itself is ruthless – events happen the way it dictates as it joins up. But the Professor has tried hard to aid the user of his dimension. He cannot dictate how the net will force its way through the dimension – that is, the events that will happen, the route it will take through all he knows – but he put in as many safety features as he could for any circumstances he could think of.

'Remember that – there will always be a way, it will always be possible, no matter what is asked of you. And the net will try and force you through routes you might think are impossible, but it is useless to try other ways. You just end up spiralling and twining and getting rammed back into another path to the same route.

'I have been here before, but there will be different routes every time, things I have not encountered. It's like a labyrinth, you see, like someone's mind; you never know what will come next. But I have never, never heard of a whole bunch of – well, outsiders – doing this. The net has forced this. It must be the only way a complete repair is possible.'

He shook his head in disbelief.

'But how will all of this – *us* – how will that affect everything? What reason can there be? The skull and us, in the house – we're, we're not important,' said Helen.

'Now, that may not become apparent for some time,' Johan admitted. 'For years even. But one thing seems to be vital. It had to be all of you. You say that you slipped dimension when Chris walked into the room, is that right?'

'If you mean, got blown into the middle of next week, yes, that's when it happened,' said Iz, still indignant.

'It must have been a shock,' said Johan. 'You see, I can

choose to do it when I want to. Some people can. Dimension slippers and sliders. Occasionally you meet them. Like your Miss Ermine, for example.'

'Miss Ermine!' said Helen as they all reeled under the impact of this news which had been delivered so matter-of-factly. They all looked at Mia. Mia blinked and looked back steadily, not saying anything.

'Don't tell me you didn't know?' asked Johan, looking equally amazed. 'I mean, dimension shifters can be quite subtle, I know. But surely you noticed?'

'Noticed – like what?' asked Helen, still at a loss.

'Well – didn't she sometimes seem to know about things that had happened when she wasn't actually there? Or – er – well, seem to not be there sometimes when you thought she was?'

They all thought for a moment. Helen was the first to speak.

'Well, I did think it was weird how she'd just vanished when we turned the corner back in the house. That was why I went back to look for Iz and Joe. But I just thought she was trying to detach a bit from Mia.' She looked slightly guiltily at Mia as she spoke. She probably wasn't supposed to tell her – but the rules seemed to be all a bit pointless, here.

'Was she in on all this, then?' asked Joe suddenly.

'Not to our knowledge, no. She won't have had the faintest idea. But after she arrived – well, you can't keep things from a dimension shifter. I reckon she did 'vanish', as you say, Helen, for just that innocent reason – trying to let Mia be a bit more free. But where she went – that's another question. I suspect she was having a protective little look around.'

'So are you saying she could have stopped this happening to us?' demanded Iz.

'No, just hampered it a bit and slowed it up.' Johan yawned. 'I didn't want to come when they asked me to, a year ago. But they got me in the end.'

'You said the others are net-fixers,' said Iz suddenly, narrowing his eyes at Johan. 'Who are you then? Why did they drag you into it?'

'I'm a simple dimension shifter. That's all. I'm quite happy minding my own business and studying sheep. Strangely, they might mess about with all this net-fixing and interrupting people's lives, but they don't seem very understanding about people. Or much outside of their own jobs. They can't do dimension shifting. Admittedly, it is born, not made. But after that it's skill, learning to handle it and use it. They just don't have it.'

'You said you didn't want to come. What made you come in the end then?' asked Helen.

'There's not time to explain now,' said Johan, 'we don't know how long we've got, and I have to tell you how we're going to get through this.'

'Will we run out of oxygen or something?' asked Joe, alarmed.

'No, but the dimension will close in again. Then we have to make decisions, quick, accurate decisions.'

'The dimension closes in?' asked Helen. 'Is that the blur? It did that to us on the edge of the brook.'

'That's right. The blur is simply the edge of the dimension. The edge of reality. You have to keep moving onwards. There are choices, though. But if you don't make them in time, you will be shoved – and you might not like where you're shoved.'

'What if we don't want to?' said Iz sulkily, bored with listening and talking. 'What if we just go our own way? I don't want to be part of some loopy experiment. I think you're talking rubbish, anyway. Show me the way out, and I'm off.' He got to his feet.

Joe looked at him. Why was he always so angry? Fear, he thought. Iz hates being frightened. And Iz hates being told what to do, that he has no choice.

Johan stood up quickly, the rest of them doing the same.

'Iz, wait, it's important you listen. There will be difficult – er – challenges ahead. We must go through as a group. If we get through them all together, we'll get out of here, I promise, and everything will be as it should be.'

'You keep saying "if", Johan,' Iz pointed out. 'What happens if not?'

'Same as anywhere else. Same as life. Make the wrong decision and – well, it's either a heck of a lot of inconvenience, or, um, you die.'

Johan said this in an off-hand way, but the impact was lost on no one.

'Did you just say, die?' squeaked Joe.

Iz turned and looked at him.

'Up to you, Joe. Stick around with the guy who's eaten too many magic mushrooms or come with me and get out of here. I'm off.' And he turned and stamped out of the only exit, another archway cut into the rock.

CHAPTER ELEVEN

'Oh hell,' said Johan. 'We'd better get after him. He'll probably kill us all if we don't.'

None of them bothered to ask him what he meant – they were getting used to baffling and fantastic statements. They also did not bother to question the fact that the archway through which they'd entered the cave had disappeared as if it had never been there. The archway on the opposite wall, through which Iz had disappeared, was now the only way out.

They hurried through after Johan, then pulled up abruptly.

They still seemed to be in some kind of cave, but this one was huge. In fact, the most striking thing about it were the great old oaks growing up and up, almost filling it with trunk and branch.

It was all wrong, thought Helen. If trees were growing in the cave, there should be a hole to the sky in the top. She tilted back her head and gazed upwards, but all she could see was a canopy of green leaves, with sparkling light glittering through like late summer sun. Mia turned her face up to the light, and turned slowly on the spot, as if spellbound. She couldn't make out a roof. But she couldn't see a sky either.

'Johan, can you climb these and get out?' she asked.

'You could certainly try. But where is out?' smiled Johan. 'I've always found that going straight forwards and through every obstacle is the only way which works.'

'What happens if you don't?' asked Joe.

'There'll just be another obstacle, or probably more. It'll be just as dangerous, and take longer in the end,' said Johan, in the weary voice of someone who'd tried it and knew.

'OK,' said Chris, then added, 'No sign of Iz. Time business coming into play again, I suppose. He should have only been a step ahead of us. You said dangerous, Johan, but this doesn't look too bad. Do we just have to walk under the trees and out the other side?'

'Well, yes, but it always pays to take a little time and a closer look,' said Johan. Looking back at the trees, he groaned, 'Obviously not Iz's approach.'

'What?' asked Helen nervously. 'I can't see anything. Just a few toadstools – oh my God!'

Before their eyes, great brown fungi were growing, pushing up through the leaf mould beneath the trees. They stood aghast as huge stalks bulged and sepia coloured flat tops spread out. They were aware of a creaking sound as the things heaved and spread, and a damp, rotting smell wafted to them on the disturbed air.

The creaking and groaning petered out. The fungi, now packed tightly together in clumps before them, seemed to have reached their final height – on a level with their faces.

'Everyone *please* keep very still,' said Johan. No one had a particular urge to move. He licked his lips nervously.

'Now, I will show you something which you'll find very useful. I hope it works for you. Any one of you – or all of you – just close your eyes for a moment and think hard about this problem in front of you. It would be better if you had more information, wouldn't it? If you could see what was going to happen? Think about needing that information. Think . . . there! There it is! Open your eyes and look.'

Floating in the air in front of Helen was something like a see-through tray.

'Helen – well done. You obviously had a strong will and a good imagination. Look in it, everyone. Come on, gather round.' Johan leant over Helen's shoulder and they all peered at the tray. It began to tilt until it was upright, facing them.

'Wow!' said Chris, 'it's like a plasma screen or something. How the heck . . . ?'

'Shhh,' said Johan, 'see? You think you see through it to the trees and the fungi, but now – now – there! They are on the screen.'

They all gave a little gasp of wonderment. The image was very beautiful, somehow, sparkling and slightly transparent as it floated in front of them.

'Now, Helen, as it has appeared closest to you, I want you to operate it,' said Johan.

Helen flashed him a worried look.

'It's OK, it's easy. As easy as thinking. Think "Scenario".'

As he was speaking, Johan cast a quick glance over his shoulder. Helen hardly noticed. She was concentrating.

The picture in front of their eyes changed in a flash. The trees were there, but they could only make out the fungi if they stared closely; faint, pale blobs smaller than a hand amongst the rich blackened brown of the leaf mould, in the shade of the great trees.

'That's how it was when we got here!' said Joe.

'Yes,' said Johan, 'I think it's running through a previous scenario first.' He glanced quickly over his shoulder again. Joe stared at the image.

'Flipping heck, it's Iz!'

They saw their friend appearing suddenly on the screen in front of the trees. With barely a pause of surprise, he stamped beneath them, hands stuffed angrily into his pockets, kicking out as he went, and disappeared behind the trunk of the most distant tree.

'The trouble is,' said Johan gently, 'he's spread the fungi. He kicked them over. That was very foolish.'

The screen changed again. Now the image was more like a diagram in a book, not a video shot.

'What the heck is *that?*' Helen asked. 'It looks like a tree, but it seems to be growing under the earth instead of on top of it. And are those some kind of fruit?'

'That's the fungi,' said Chris suddenly. 'Or rather, the whole damn thing is the fungus, and what we are seeing here, in front of us, are just the – well, like the tips of branches, flowers, fruit, whatever you want to call it. The real heart of it is underground, as big as these flipping trees.'

'Then it's like one thing, not lots,' said Joe, wonderingly. 'Crikey. That's quite scary. I bet they're poisonous. They don't look like mushrooms, do they?'

There was a tiny, audible 'ping' and a skull and crossbones appeared on the top left-hand corner of the screen.

'Poison,' said Mia automatically.

'Very helpful of it,' said Chris with sarcasm. 'Is that just if you eat it, I wonder, or if you touch it?'

'Shhh, watch,' said Helen, 'it's changing again.'

The screen returned to the original scene of trees and leaf mould. This time they could see the scattered, fallen fungus, and realised they were watching events after Iz had passed through on his destructive path. Suddenly, more pale bulbs appeared above ground; magically, they grew, thrusting upwards, until they crammed the space beneath the trees.

What will happen if we try to get through? thought Helen. Does it matter if you touch them, like Chris said? Perhaps . . .

'Wow,' said Joe, 'there's us! We're walking through— oh!'

They had seen themselves, just for a moment, heading into the clumps. Then suddenly the screen changed to a digitalised, representational outline picture. They recognised themselves shown as merely white circles moving through clear brown outlines which seemed to be the fungus shoots. One of the white circles bounced into a brown outline. It shook, and strange black dots appeared to fire out in all directions from the open cap. The poison icon in the top corner of the screen flashed and repeated its 'ping' sound. The white circles turned red, then disappeared.

They turned and looked simultaneously at Johan in horror.

'What – what was that? What did it mean?' said Helen.

'It's all right,' said Johan. 'It can't show you the future. That's why it's not a real picture. You just asked it for a scenario prediction – it's very useful. Saves you making dangerous mistakes.'

'The spores,' said Chris, 'the spores are deadly, aren't they?'

'Certainly looks like it,' said Johan, 'which is why I wanted to guide you all through together. I wanted to show you how to use this first. And now –' he looked over his shoulder again, 'and now we're just about out of time, I'm afraid.'

They turned as one, and looked behind them. Instead of the archway and the stone walls of the cave, there was just a blur, and it was moving towards them, swallowing ground slowly but surely.

'No!' Helen shouted, then stared at Johan. He gazed back steadily with his caramel-coloured eyes. 'Johan! Can't you stop this? It's not a game. We could be killed!'

'You know I can't. And if we don't move soon, it'll simply push us into the fungi,' he shrugged.

'The screen,' said Chris urgently. 'Can't we try out more scenarios and see what works?'

'Well, we could,' said Johan, 'except now there's no time. Which is a downer, I know. So we'll have to just go for it as best we can. I think we stand more chance under our own steam than being rammed through, don't you?'

Exasperated, Chris stared at him and then away at the trees and the fungi. Could you climb through the branches? One glance showed him that none of the branches grew so conveniently. Gaps too wide to cross. Risk of falling.

'Come on, quick, everyone,' he said suddenly, and looked at Johan, who nodded. 'We can get through. It's just, we must be very careful not to knock any.'

'Oh hell,' said Joe.

'What *now?*'

'I'm bigger than you. Across, at least. And I'm clumsy.

Everyone knows that,' said Joe sadly. 'You'd better all go first so when I hit one, it doesn't reach you too.'

Joe felt Mia's eyes on him, and turned to look at her questioningly. Then he remembered.

'Oh, Christ, and Mia. She can't do it either. She could hardly get across the landing net. She says her hands don't do what she tells them, and I guess that goes for the rest of her body. Is that right, Mia?'

'That is correct,' said Mia formally, with a little bow of her head.

'The blur!' said Helen. 'Oh hurry, it's closing in! If it bounces us, we'll definitely hit the damn things. Oh, I hate this. What the heck are we going to do about Mia? Joe, you're just being silly. I don't believe you've got anything wrong with you. You won't be clumsy if you just try. Come on, your life depends on it. Maybe all our lives.'

'That's all you can do, Joe,' said Johan sympathetically, 'try really hard. And Mia, I suppose.'

'No!' said Joe. 'That's not fair. Mia really did try, on the net. She couldn't help it. Look, I'll carry her on my back if I have to.'

Chris stared at him, wrestling with some emotion.

'Get in there, get going,' he shouted suddenly, giving him a shove towards the fungi. 'You said yourself you're clumsy. You'll never manage her as well. I'll blinking well take her. GO ON!'

Joe looked at the trees and fungus heads and saw that now the area looked like a forest clearing in the middle of nowhere. The walls of the cave all around and behind had disappeared into the blur. He couldn't see beyond the thick stems to the other side, but trusted there was some way out.

Helen was already edging sideways past the first great stems, shoulder first, the other shoulder touching the trunk of one of the trees. Johan was just behind her, looking back at the others.

Joe took a step forwards, then said, 'All the same, you go first, Chris. I still think I might knock one.'

'Whatever,' said Chris, then turned to Mia. 'Come on, you. Can you get on my back?'

'Yes,' she answered, but stood, gazing at him.

'Well then?' he shouted, as the blur edged towards them. 'What are you waiting for? Get on, quick.'

Joe paused, went back to Mia's side.

'Mia, like a hug. Look – just like a hug, only hug his back not his front. See?' He demonstrated by clambering slightly on to Chris's back.

'Oh my God, is she dense or what?' Chris protested. 'Joe, you weigh a ton. Get off, would you? If she doesn't want a lift, I'll go without her.'

'No, no, Chris, don't be horrible. She just – she just doesn't think like us, that's all. She can do it. Can't you, Mia?'

Mia was looking at Chris with undisguised distaste, but, copying Joe, started to climb on to Chris's back. As Chris hooked his arms under her denim-clad legs she squirmed in discomfort.

'Safe,' said Joe clearly, 'now you are safe. But you MUSTN'T TOUCH the nasty plant things, Mia. Do you understand?'

'Yes,' said Mia, as if he were slightly stupid for mentioning it.

Chris headed towards the first opening he could see between two fungus stems, steadied as he judged the distance.

'Can you keep your feet in, Mia?' he said.

'No,' said Mia calmly.

'What do you mean, no?'

'No. They go that way.'

Chris made a little explosive sound, then, trying to keep his elbows crooked around the girl's upper legs, he felt down with his hands. Finding the hard leather of her boots, he managed to grab both of her feet, turned out almost at right angles. Holding them firmly, he pulled her toes until they were pointing forwards. He heard no sound of complaint. He felt her elbows around his neck, her head pressed against the side of his face, her long hair on his cheek. Hopefully nothing else was sticking out.

'OK, sit still now.'

He pressed on, past the stem, leaning to the left to avoid the edge of the cap which almost touched his shoulder. Now another in front, and hardly enough room between it and its neighbour, but the only way to go . . . on, lean to the right, almost – there, done it, and now where?

Joe followed them as the blur almost touched his heel. He felt worried about Mia, disappointed that Chris had had to do what he felt he should have done. The least he could do was keep an eye on them. He called out, 'Bit more to the left, Chris. That's it. Watch the one on your right, there. Mind her toe – it's nearly touching the smaller one, near your waist. On the left . . .'

'Thanks, mate,' Chris called back. 'Can you keep telling me? I can't see that well, her legs are in the way and I can't turn my head.'

'OK, just let me keep up,' said Joe breathlessly, sliding sideways between two stalks. He sucked in his stomach, pulled in his backside. These were very tall, the caps pressed together over his head. Droplets of sticky-looking moisture trickled slowly, like clear treacle, down the deathly beige skin of the stem in front of his nose. The reek of earth, of rot, of death, rose into his nostrils, poured over his throat. He could taste it.

A slight sob of disgust escaped him. He looked upwards and saw the dark, burnt-looking underside of the cap hanging over him, the dull plaster pink of the gills radiating out, with their invisible, deadly burden waiting to be released at the smallest vibration.

'Left OK, Joe? Joe? Am I OK to the left?'

It was Chris's voice. Joe realised he had stopped moving, was standing stock still. He pulled himself together.

'Hang on a bit, Chris. Just coming,' he called and stepped carefully sideways until he was out from between the stems and standing in a small space between several more. Chris and Mia were just to one side of him - he could see only their backs.

'There's no small ones, you're OK. Just the two on either side. When you're through, I think I can see a smaller one you might catch with your hip, on the right. But you can see that, can't you?'

'Yep, got that. Thanks, Joe.'

Joe looked down at his hands for a moment, and checked

which was the one he used for writing. He wondered at the way he'd just said 'Left' and 'Right' like that. He normally wasn't too sure.

They pushed on, and though it seemed like a terrible maze, sometimes making them veer to the right or left, they never lost their bearings. They could tell which way was straight on – perhaps because of the position of the trees, Joe thought.

The effort of concentrating was starting to make him sweat. He wiped droplets as they reached his eyebrows, desperate to keep his eyes clear. He remembered to keep his elbows in to his sides as he did so. The thing to do was to keep yourself like a tight, tied-up parcel, he thought. With a very bendy bit in the middle, he added, as he ducked cautiously under another cap. As he looked, he saw it unfurl just a fraction more. Clearing it, he saw Chris and Mia facing him, Chris dropping Mia unceremoniously whilst gazing at Joe. There were no stalks anywhere near them. Disbelievingly, Joe straightened up, checking all around.

He saw Johan a few paces away, and Helen, slapping her hands on her thighs with delight.

'You did it! You did it! Joe! Well done!'

'Well done Chris, more like,' said Joe, walking towards them and stretching his arms out from his sides. They were still in a cave, apparently, still lit with the same gentle glow from above, but there were no blurred edges.

'I already said that,' said Helen, 'and well done the lot of us.' And she grabbed Joe as he joined them and hugged him furiously.

'But I didn't get one of those,' said Chris.

'Oh, one for you too,' said Helen, grinning widely, and clamped her arms around him in turn.

Johan stood back, smiling, and Mia tweaked and pulled her clothes straight in her pernickety way.

'One down,' said Johan, 'but quite a few to go. Ah, here's our friend Iz.'

And there he was, looking uncertainly at them, hands in pockets, scraping the ground around with his shoe.

Chris's reaction took them all by surprise.

'You complete dork! You flipping moron, Iz!' he bristled, arms stiff by his sides, fists clenched. 'Why do you always have to go storming off like that? Don't you learn? You've caused nothing but trouble with your flipping moods. Like a bloody prima donna bloody ballerina!'

Iz wasn't sure what that last bit meant, but he did catch the bit about ballerinas. The colour rushed to his face and he took on the same posture as the other boy.

'Did you call me a flipping *queer?*' he snarled.

This only made Chris falter for a second.

'God, Iz, you *are* stupid. I'm talking about storming off when you don't know what you're doing, when someone has offered to help. You nearly *killed* us all!'

'What? I—'

'You kicked over all the fungi. Then they shot up like you see now. They're full of poisonous spores. They only didn't get you because they were tiny when you went through. We could all have walked around them easy as pie if you hadn't booted through like a clumsy git.'

'It wasn't my fault,' began Iz defensively, but got no further. Chris flew at him, and a punch from his fist sent Iz flying back on to the dirt of the cave floor. In a second, he was back on his feet, fists whirling. There was a scuffle, then both stood back for a moment and glared at each other, Iz with an ugly red mark on his jaw, Chris with a trickle of blood from the corner of his lip.

It had all happened so quickly that the others had barely had time to react. Now Joe realised that they were pausing to size each other up. He did the same. Chris was larger than Iz, not taller, but handy-looking. This could be interesting.

Helen was horrified.

'Chris! Iz! No, stop it!' Then, correctly anticipating that she would be ignored, she turned to Johan. 'Johan! Make them stop it, for God's sake!' Seeing Johan standing with folded arms, looking heavenwards, she appealed instead to Joe.

'Joe! He's your friend. Stop him!'

'Well, I could try,' said Joe calmly, watching as the two boys circled each other, crouched, fists up, 'but I've never managed it yet.'

'Oh, they'll be all right,' said Johan lazily. 'I would point out the issue of time, however. You never know down here. We might be shunted along any minute now. And into what?'

'Did you hear that?' shouted Helen, whirling to face the combatants, her hair flying around behind her and ending up half over her face. She swept it back angrily with her hand. 'I said, DID – YOU – HEAR – THAT?'

Slowly, eyes flickering to the angry figure standing with hands on hips, the two boys stopped circling and lowered their hands.

'All right then. All right. Another time, though,' hissed Iz through his teeth at Chris.

'Any time,' said Chris casually, with an arrogant tilt to his head.

'Right,' said Johan, 'everybody ready? Then on we go.' And he turned and led the way, to where the cave narrowed into a tunnel, and one by one, they followed.

CHAPTER TWELVE

The tunnel was quite wide and well-lit, like a corridor. Rather subdued, they walked along behind Johan.

'It's all right, Iz,' said Joe, pleased to be with his friend again and wanting him to be less miserable. 'No one really blames you, not for everything, you know.'

Iz hunched his shoulders. 'Yes they do. Right from the start. I always get the blame. And I know I went in the room, but I didn't make everyone follow me, did I? Nor down the brook.'

'No, I know. No one's really saying you did. It's just, there isn't anyone else to blame right here. *You* wanted to blame someone, remember, and you picked on Johan, and he's said it isn't down to him. I suppose it's the Professor, at the end of the day.'

'Yeah, I suppose so.' Iz kicked gloomily at a small stone.

Helen looked back as she heard the slight sound. She saw Iz's downcast face and hung back for a moment, waiting for him.

'All right, sunshine?' she asked, with a cautious smile.

'Mmm,' said Iz.

'Not being horrible, Iz, but I wish you'd get out of that habit of kicking things, just while we're down here. You never know what you'll set off.'

Iz saw the sense in what she said, and let the stone rest where it was as he passed it.

Joe pushed him in the arm affectionately.

'Probably set off an earthquake or something, Iz.'

His friend looked up from under his fringe and managed a small smile. None of them could laugh about it properly – it seemed all too likely, too possible, down here.

'Nobody's saying you did it on purpose, Iz,' said Helen. 'Only, it seems that when you don't think, it all comes back on us, whether you mean it to or not.'

'I know, it's just I'm used to doing what I want. Alone. Anyway, I still feel bad, don't I? I mean, about Joe, and all of you – except that prat Chris – I might have killed you. Even if I didn't mean to, it comes as a bit of a shock.'

It was as close to an apology as you were likely to get from Iz, Joe thought.

'You are funny, Iz,' said Helen in surprise. 'If I'd have been you, and did what you did, and felt like that afterwards, I think the first thing I'd have done when I saw everyone appear safe and well was jump about for joy. And say sorry.'

'I knew everyone would be mad with me,' was all Iz muttered by way of explanation.

Helen became rather brisk.

'Well, you won't make things better for everyone by staying all moody. Come on, Iz, you seemed to have lots of fight in you just now with Chris. We've got to fight on and get through this.' She aimed some little punches in the air towards Iz.

'Mmm,' said Iz again. He wished it was just a case of a good old scrap with something real, something you could get your hands on.

They were approaching the end of the tunnel, it seemed, and the wide opening to yet another cave. Johan, Chris and Mia were, by now, a little way ahead of them, and they heard Mia say distinctly, 'Pretty. Balloons.' Then she paused, and as they arrived behind her, she added, '*Not* balloons. *Not* bubbles. *Like* bubbles. Pretty.'

Johan and Chris stepped aside to allow the others a view.

'Oh my – oh Lordy,' said Helen softly.

The entire floor of the cave was taken up with a sunken pool, made of glass set down in the ground so that only a slight lip remained above. It was only as deep as a normal swimming pool – you could tell, because the water was quite clear and you could see to the bottom. Floating gently over the surface were numerous, large, domed shapes, transparent yet gleaming with iridescence. Below the umbrella-shaped domes hung coils and tendrils in great masses, almost touching the bottom of the pool in places.

'Jellyfish,' said Johan.

'Portuguese man-o'-war,' added Chris, authoratively.

'Actually, I think they're a pretty undiscovered type of box jellyfish, Chris,' corrected Johan with a polite cough.

'Not as bad?' asked Chris, but with a slightly hopeless note.

'Man-o'-war get a rather unfair press. They're not as bad . . .'

'As these, you mean,' said Helen with a sigh. 'Why don't you just come out with it, Johan? They're flipping lethal, aren't they?'

'Well, yes, I think so, pretty much. Not my speciality. But

at the least they'd probably do terrible damage, even if you managed to get to hospital in time.'

'Which doesn't seem very likely, given our current situation,' put in Chris.

'We must watch the time,' said Joe worriedly. 'We're standing about here talking. We need that screen thingy.'

'What screen thingy?' asked Iz.

'It's bloody good. Isn't it, Johan?' Joe appealed.

'Useful,' Johan agreed. 'You still have to get through though, when all's said and done. Give it a try.'

'Helen should do it. Go on, Helen. She was best,' said Joe.

Helen looked worried as they all turned to look at her.

'Well, I–'

'If you remember,' Johan interrupted, 'you all tried. It just came up closest to Helen because she was strongest with the signal. And when each of you thought of a possibility, it responded. That means you get the most out of it if you use *all* your minds, which think in rather different ways.'

It made sense. Iz was restless for action.

'Come on, then, Joe's right. We need to get a move on. I haven't been bounced anywhere yet, and I don't want to be bounced into that lot. Tell me how to do it.'

Johan explained again, with a few interruptions from Helen. Now they were all looking over their shoulders, as Johan had done in the previous cave.

'Eyes shut,' said Helen. 'Think "Scenario". Think.'

Joe looked doubtfully at Mia. What did that mean to her? he wondered. He wouldn't normally know big or weird words like that; it just so happened it had come up in a PC war game he'd played. Mia wasn't closing her eyes, either. He felt that probably didn't matter. Such strange eyes. Mia didn't always seem to be seeing, anyway. Or not seeing what everyone else was.

'Think, you want to know about the jellyfish, Mia,' said Joe. 'Think, how do we get through without being touched by them?'

She flicked her eyes sideways at him and then stared ahead again at the pool. He hoped it had worked.

'Come on, Joe, stop blabbing. Concentrate,' said Iz.

All except Mia closed their eyes. Then they heard Johan's voice.

'You've got it.'

Iz opened his eyes and took a step backwards. Something see-through was floating in front of him, and for a second, he connected it to the jellyfish and was afraid.

'OK, Iz, you've got it. Can everyone see?'

They nodded, waited as it tilted, turning upright in front of them until they could see the pool through it. Steadily, the image grew stronger until it was on the screen in front of them.

'Oh, neat!' said Iz, his amazement overcoming his wariness. 'If only I could have one of these to game on. Perhaps they'll make one, one day. Wouldn't that be something?'

Johan opened his mouth as if to say something, then closed it again.

'What?' said Joe, who'd noticed.

'Nothing, nothing. Come on, ask questions. Precise ones. It's no good trying "how do we get through?".'

'Could we kill them?' asked Iz.

The screen changed to the graphic, representational one they had seen before. The pool was a three-dimensional suggestion of simple blue lines, the ground line shown in brown. The jellyfish were shown as red oval shapes. There were rather a lot of them, they realised – they covered about half of the surface of the pool and were spread about all over it. There was the 'ping' sound, and a little icon which looked rather like a pirate's cutlass appeared in the bottom right-hand corner of the screen. A red diagonal line then appeared over the top of it.

'I guess that means you've no weapons. Is that right, Johan?' said Joe.

Johan nodded.

Helen looked at the pool before them.

'With those dangly things, I don't suppose we can squeeze between them like the fungi? They pretty much cover the space, spread out like that. And they move too.'

The screen immediately showed white circles lined up by the pool. One moved into the pool. The movement seemed to cause the red oval nearest to be pushed away, creating a knock-on effect, with all the ovals moving around. In a second, the white circle had been bounced into by several; it turned red and disappeared.

'Those white things are us,' explained Joe to Iz. 'It's doing that because Helen thought about it, you see.'

'Hmm,' said Iz, staring intently. He looked up at Johan. 'We are sure these are deadly, are we?'

Almost before he'd finished the question, they heard the 'ping' from the screen, and were not surprised to see the skull and crossbones icon had appeared again.

'Poison,' said Mia, sounding, Helen thought, irritatingly pleased with herself.

'And a really horrible agonising death, if it's like other jellyfish I've read about,' added Chris gloomily.

'They would cover only half the pool if they would just shove over a bit,' said Joe.

'A net would be good, like the shark nets they use off beaches in Australia,' said Chris, 'to protect the swimmers. We went there last year to visit my uncle.'

No scene change happened on the screen. They glanced around at the walls and floor of the cave.

'No net,' said Iz. 'Typical. All this lot on about nets and they can't leave a useful bit about when we want it. And we can't get back to the one we bounced in on.'

'They look like they'd blow over into one half of the pool, if there was a bit of a current or a wind,' said Joe, 'but that's not likely down here. If we tried to splash them over, you know, make a wave, I think they'd just go all over the place, like in the first scene the screen showed us.'

'It's no good thinking of things we know *won't* work,' said Helen. 'The screen doesn't even bother to run through them. It's not changed for ages. We're losing time. We should be asking *good* questions.'

They all frowned, thinking hard. Helen felt she should come up with something as she'd made the criticism, but her mind was a blank.

'Ask them to move?'

It was the strange accent of Mia which broke the silence, with the emphasis on all the wrong words.

They looked at her blankly.

'That's what I had to learn. You can't push people around. Mustn't point. Mustn't pull. You must speak to them.'

She actually looks shy, thought Joe. I don't think I've ever seen her look – well, anything much. Except cross maybe.

Mia looked away, back at the pool.

'But these aren't people, Mia,' said Helen gently. 'Still, it's an idea. Maybe you can communicate with them somehow.'

Suddenly, the screen changed.

'Look!' said Helen, 'she might be on to something.'

But the screen seemed to have gone quite mad. An icon which looked like a lightning bolt appeared in blue at the top. Then the whole viewing area filled with numbers, which whirled and changed frantically as if undergoing some huge computation.

'Johan, what's going on? Has it gone crazy?' asked Helen, starting to glance around for the blurring of the walls.

'Looks like a virus or something,' said Chris.

Johan stared at the screen over their shoulders.

'Wait a moment, give it a chance,' he said. 'The icon at the top means communication is possible. But . . .' He paused.

The screen had almost entirely filled with red ovals, now very tiny but very densely packed. They were circled in blue.

'Right. The blue circle means benign. That means, the individual doesn't actually mean to do you any harm.'

'But does that mean we can wade through touching them, and they will make sure they don't sting us? And why are there so many of them on the screen now? In the real pool, there's no more than before,' gabbled Helen, checking rapidly and then looking back to the screen. 'I hope they aren't going to do what the fungi did.'

'I'm afraid they don't have a choice about stinging you,' said Johan. 'The tendrils just dangle there and they can't switch off the stinging cells – a bit like a nettle. The tentacles carry on stinging you even if they aren't attached any more. They can pull up the tentacles, but they don't *choose* to do so – it just happens automatically when prey is caught, to bring the food in.'

'So they don't want to hurt us, necessarily, but can't do much about it,' said Iz, 'and communication is possible, so – so I suppose we can ask them to bomb into one half of the pool sharpish, at least. Why are there so many on the screen though, Johan?'

'I'm afraid – um, well, you can only communicate with each individual one at a time, and it appears that there are rather a lot of individuals to talk to. I think I know why. Each jellyfish isn't actually one being – it's a collection of creatures joined together to make the whole thing. Each one has its special job, and all acting together, they can exist very well. But there isn't one big brain in charge which you can talk to and which tells all the other ones what to do.'

'That's very weird,' said Helen. 'I can't imagine it. Do you mean, the tentacles are one creature, the top bit is another?'

'The cells. Every cell a separate individual,' said Johan quietly.

'We're made up of cells,' said Chris, 'but I suppose it's different. Being as we have brains and nerve endings joining up and so on.'

'If they've all got different jobs, it's more like we're looking at a colony, not a creature, isn't it?' said Iz. 'Like an ant's nest, or bees?'

'Mmm,' said Johan, 'one way of looking at it. Scientists have begun to question where it all ends. You never know. Maybe people are just like cells of one big organism.'

'So we can't really talk to them all, one at a time, can we?' Helen said practically. 'And if we did, they can't necessarily talk to each other and make a movement away, even just one jellyfish. That would take ages.'

'That is the downside,' said Johan, gazing at the jellyfish with a romantic, faraway look in his eyes, 'of a system which some people call primitive, but some of us like to think of as beautifully simple. After all, it's done well for them for thousands of years.'

'That's as may be,' said Joe, 'but all of this is getting us no further. We'll run out of time soon. Give us a clue, for God's sake, Johan. You seem to know an awful lot of stuff, and we're struggling about with this flipping screen, and you could tell us all this stuff much quicker.'

'I can tell you about jellyfish. But I don't know how to get through this any more than you do. I might put you on the wrong scent entirely. I might kill you all. The net is causing this challenge – it's challenging *you*, all of you. I believe that's why you're here – not just to tag along and do what I say,' he said. 'I don't mind interpreting what you bring up on the screen. I can't just lead you through, much as I'd like to. You have to work out the best way. It's not all that great for me, remember. I have to go along with your methods, even though they might kill me.'

'Just a suggestion, or a hint then?' pleaded Iz. Johan looked at him in surprise.

'I thought you – oh, never mind. All I can say is, think about what you do know. Whatever you've learnt off TV, at school, through books – and then try from there.'

'Don't think they do jellyfish in Science, do they, Chris?'

said Iz, addressing the other boy as if they had never had a fight.

'Well, we haven't in our class. What about in yours?'

'Don't really go to it. TV – I'm sure I've seen them on a programme. But I can't think of anything else. When they want to move somewhere, what makes them go? Do they just drift about hoping food turns up? Could we drop some food down one end of the pool?'

The screen remained stubbornly unchanging.

'No food, I suppose. It might at least put up a little fishfood tub with a line through it,' sighed Iz.

'I think like Joe said, they get blown and go on currents. But there could be other things that affect them. I mean, you don't get them everywhere. You don't get them in our sea, do you?' said Chris, thinking out loud. 'It must be too cold. This tank must be heated!'

'Aha!' said Helen. 'Could we just turn off the heater?'

'That would be pretty cruel, Helen,' said Joe reprovingly. 'I mean, they don't want to do us any harm. They didn't ask us to come barging along to cross their pool. And Johan said they weren't even really discovered yet, or something, didn't you, Johan? They're probably rare.'

Johan nodded.

Helen looked at Joe in amazement.

'You are the weirdest boy . . .' she said, but was interrupted by Iz before she could say any more.

'Look – the screen's changing.'

There was a 'ping', and a red line drawn under the blue line showing the bottom of the pool suddenly turned grey.

'I think that's the heating element off,' said Chris. 'I

wonder how long it takes to cool the water down to the level where they die off?'

Immediately, figures appeared on the screen.

'A centigrade an hour – that's slow,' read Chris. 'And what the hell's an hour down here anyway? What's the lowest temperature they can survive at?'

More figures appeared. Joe looked away, disagreeing with the turn this was taking.

'Uh, it's at 35 at the moment – they can cope with 17,' said Iz, peering. 'That's a heck of a wait.'

'No good anyway,' said Mia, 'I know. I can see. Watch the screen.'

They looked at her in surprise, and then glanced at the screen. The temperature reading showed 15. The red ovals turned pale blue. Again, the white circles lined up, and one moved into the pool. Exactly the same happened as in the first attempt, except that this time the ovals shuffling around and bumping were no longer red – all the same, the white circle once again turned red and disappeared.

Iz said something crude.

Joe looked at the screen, puzzled.

'You did that, Mia? What does it mean?'

'Still sting. They still sting. Dead,' said Mia seriously.

'You knew that,' said Johan to the rest of them, 'if you just thought. I told you, the tentacles sting even when they're cut off. We really are going to have to make a decision quickly.'

They looked over their shoulders to where Johan was looking, knowing but dreading what they would see. The cave walls behind them had begun to fade. They looked quickly back at the screen.

'Last chance,' said Chris. 'Now, we didn't pay enough attention to the diagram. That red line showing the heating element was there the whole time, and we never asked what it was. Let's just check there's nothing else. I mean, there might be a slide-out cover or something. Then we'd look pretty silly.'

They stared hard at the screen, but could see nothing resembling a cover. Helen pointed at a tiny light bulb symbol she hadn't noticed before, above the image of the pool.

'What's that?'

They looked at the real pool. There was light shining down, sparkling on the floating creatures below. They had just assumed it was the same natural glow they had encountered the whole time they'd been down here.

Iz put his hand to his brow, shielding his eyes as he stared upwards.

'Can't see very well what's making it. Could it be a lighting rig? What do you reckon Joe? Johan, is that likely?'

'Could be,' said Johan, looking up at the light as if he, too, had never noticed it before.

'Quick, the blur is closing in again,' said Helen. Already the archway through which they had entered and the ground behind them was disappearing. She glanced back at the screen.

'The light – it can't be just to keep them warm, like chickens,' said Joe bafflingly, 'they have the element for that. They must like it, or need it for something.'

Helen thought for a moment. A light could only be off or on, couldn't it? What happens if it goes off? she thought.

The bulb on the screen turned black. The ovals, which had turned red again after their previous experiment with temperature, sank as one to the bottom of the pool.

'Well,' said Iz, 'it's an idea. But we'd have to swim without dropping our feet down. And I wonder how you turn it off anyway?'

Joe hardly dared speak. He had asthma, and the fear of suffocation had linked itself in some strange way to water. He had learnt to swim, but he wasn't very good. He could not guarantee his feet wouldn't touch down at some point. Then there was Mia. Did she swim? If she did, did her feet do as she asked?

Iz's last question seemed to have had an effect. The screen flashed a small square, shown up high on the wall beside the pool, to the right.

'What's that mean?' he said, staring at the screen, then looking in the air over the pool.

'It looks a bit like something in a circuit diagram,' said Chris, leaning over his shoulder. 'I think it's because you asked how to turn off the lights. I think it's the lighting rig operation unit, in which case . . .' He paused, scouting around with his eyes – 'it must be on the wall or something. There!'

On the rock wall to one side of the pool was a box they had overlooked because it was almost the same sandy colour as its surroundings.

'If you weren't looking for it, you'd never see it,' said Helen softly.

Joe stepped sideways, closer to the pool.

'It's moving in, you guys. Keep out of the way.'

They all shuffled sideways, then stared at the box.

'Who's good at climbing, then?' said Johan, sounding cheerful. 'I would offer, I'm pretty good, what with clambering about up hills and mountains after sheep. But I know for a fact these walls won't take my weight.'

Helen eyed him critically. He was a pretty skinny man, she thought, if nice-looking. Joe was heavier, surely, and would say he was too clumsy to climb. Mia – no. Chris – again, as heavy as Johan, surely. Iz was probably good at climbing, and there wasn't much to him. She might just weigh in all right, though she would never be exactly slender.

'I'll do it,' said Iz.

'No, Iz, I will,' said Helen, to their surprise. 'I saw the light bulb symbol. I'd like to do it. I'm not bad at climbing and heights don't bother me at all. Just give Joe and Mia a hand, would you? You'll be more use like that.'

Helen had a way of speaking which told everyone her mind was made up. They looked at each other and decided not to argue.

'Let's get right on the edge of the pool, now, before someone gets bounced in without realising,' said Chris. 'It's tiring keeping an eye on this blur. Let's get near the edge and keep our eyes on it while Helen shimmies up the wall.'

'This could be one heck of an interesting swimming lesson,' said Iz, suddenly cheerful and presenting his back to the pool. 'Go on, Spider-woman, get up there quick and see what you can do.' He flashed Helen a quick smile.

Helen steadied herself at the base of the natural rock wall where it met the edge of the pool. She looked up. The box was about five metres above her and a couple of metres to the left, overhanging the pool. She planned the diagonal route, checking for handholds. She could see several – small rocks bulged out here and there.

'What sort of moron puts a flipping electric box right up where you can't reach it? Professor my ass . . . maybe there's a scaffolding tower or something you're supposed to use.'

The others faced the blur, with the pool and its inhabitants behind them. They could hear Helen's complaint as she scrambled up but hardly dared take their eyes from the advancing haze. They saw the screen, left floating when they moved to their new position, fade suddenly into background vagueness and disappear.

A particularly strong curse from Helen and a few little splashing sounds made them glance up at her quickly.

'OK there?' called Johan.

'Just a few stones fell out. I slipped. It is crumbly, Johan, you're right,' she called down, trying to sound confident. Her stomach was churning as she tried not to think about falling into that water. Below her she could see the delicate pearl and milk of the domes floating almost motionless. They are all relying on me, she thought. She was trying not to think ahead about switching off the light, climbing down in pitch black and entering the water. She wouldn't be able to see the blur then. It might close in on her in the dark. How long did it take for the jellyfish to sink to the bottom when the light went out? On the screen, it had looked immediate. But that was just a simulation. No one had even asked if Mia could swim. Perhaps Iz would try and tow her across. Oh God.

She looked down as her hands found the box and grabbed on tight. Here, up on the wall, she was almost over the centre of the pool, and she had more space between herself and the blur than the others below. She saw Iz looking up at her. The blur was nearly at his toes.

'No rush or anything, Helen,' he called up, then added, 'hey, why don't you ever wear a skirt? I think it would suit you, you know.'

'Ooh, Iz, you creep! If I ever get down from here . . .' Helen growled. She wedged her toes tight into the ledge she had found, gripped the box with her left hand, and grappled with what seemed to be a door or flap on the front of it. It came up suddenly from the bottom, and she realised it was hinged at the top. Inside there were switches and levers. She had no particular knowledge of electrics, she realised, and wondered if after all, she should have let Iz do this.

Iz seemed to read her mind. He looked up again.

'I'd just look for an off button, if it was me. Failing that, hit them all,' he shouted.

You would, she thought, and it would probably do something terrible. She looked closely at the contents of the box. None of the switches looked clearly like an on–off button. What did the levers do?

Suddenly, it came to her. They probably *moved* the lights. The jellyfish sank when the lights were off. That must mean they liked it, needed it, didn't it? In that case, wouldn't they follow the lights?

'Hurry, Helen!' shouted Joe. She looked down.

They were all starting to sit with one leg over the edge of the pool. The blur was about to bounce into them.

'It's OK. Hold on. I've got an idea!' she shouted back, and pulled the lever to the right.

The light at the left side of the pool seemed to go off, leaving it in darkness, and a bright glare hit the little group. They called out in horror. Helen, squinting down through the brightness, could see them trying to snatch their legs out of the water as the jellyfish crowded to their side of the pool. She realised immediately what had happened – she'd moved the lever to the right, and the lighting rig had swung the lights that way. Eyes watering from the glare, she wrenched the lever to the left. As she did so, she heard a huge splash from below. She was instantly plunged into darkness.

The left half of the pool was now brightly lit, and Helen could see the bobbing, drifting tops of the jellyfish there. She started to climb down to the water.

Joe came up spluttering in the dark, gasping in fear. He thought he felt jellyfish tentacles around his ankles and screamed out. He had been balanced on the edge of the pool a moment before, and a jellyfish had been near him, drawn by the light Helen had turned on them. And then the blur had hit him, firing him into the water and to, he believed, a certain and agonising death. When he surfaced, the light had gone. He couldn't put his feet on the bottom, but he trod water for a moment, still gasping in terror. He waited for the pain.

He heard the splashes as the others entered the water more carefully. In a moment, he felt a hand grasp his arm.

'Joe! Are you all right?'

It was Iz. There was just enough light to see his wet face streaming with damp, dark locks.

'Can't – breathe,' gasped Joe.

'You're all right, Joe. Nothing's got you. They all went to the other half of the pool when the light moved.'

Joe realised it was true. There was no searing pain. The tangly feeling round his legs was just his trousers.

'If you can talk, you can breathe,' came Johan's voice near by. 'Just get to the other side.'

'Where – where's Mia?' Joe managed to say, before a slap of water hit him in the mouth.

'Swimming across fine. I saw her. Get a move on, mate.'

They both swam for the other side, Iz grabbing his friend under one armpit every so often and shunting him. As they neared the edge, Mia was alongside them, making good headway.

They hauled themselves out, fighting the gravity of sodden, dripping clothes, feeling the thick glass edge of the pool digging into their palms, knees and ankles. They lay gasping in pools of water on the dark sandy cave floor. Mia flopped next to them.

Chris was already there and on his feet, looking worried.

'There you are! That's three of you, now where's Johan and Helen – ah, here's Johan – oh, Helen's already out.'

'Have you ever thought of being a Scout leader, Chris?' said Iz, with his best innocent and friendly dog look.

Chris looked wary.

'I *was* in the Scouts, actually. For years. Why?'

Joe interrupted. 'Did you see Mia? What the heck was that stroke?' He grinned across at her, raising himself up on his arms and still puffing.

She ignored him.

'Nothing known to man nor beast, I'd say,' said Iz. 'But by crikey, it worked.'

CHAPTER THIRTEEN

Johan shook himself like a dog, and hitched up his sodden jeans. His wet T-shirt stuck to his body, showing how skinny he really was. They all looked at each other with wet hair, seeing the strange impact it had on familiar faces.

'What the heck are we going to do? We're going to stay soaking now. We didn't exactly come equipped for this,' said Iz, wringing out the bottom of his jeans.

'You never know what's around the corner in a place like this,' said Johan mysteriously. 'I'll bet – no, come on, let's take a look first, before I say anything which might disappoint you.'

Johan strode on briskly, in a manner quite unlike his usual self. They followed less confidently, shaking a leg here, unsticking a sleeve there, Mia and Helen scraping their fingers through their long wet hair.

Round a slight bend and into the next cave and:

'There!' said Johan, punching the air and jumping round to face them, silhouetted by the great glowing fire in the centre of the cave ahead of them.

'Oh yes. Oh thank you, Johan. Oh well done,' said Iz,

diving forwards. In a matter of moments they were crouching, standing and steaming around the flickering flames. No one spoke for a while; no one asked how it was done. The flames and the heat, the logs that were burning, seemed real enough. They didn't care.

'Don't thank me,' said Johan. 'The Professor ensured the lighting rig was there, at least. Now he's made sure there's a way of drying out. I thought he might.'

Iz threw all caution to the wind, and stripped down to his underwear, holding his clothes out to the fire to dry and placing his trainers near the heat.

Chris soon did the same, and Johan just took off his T-shirt and held it out towards the glow.

'Go on, Joe, otherwise you'll never get dry properly,' urged Iz, but Joe shook his head. He couldn't possibly, not with *his* build, and girls here. 'Honestly, no one's looking,' added Iz, but without much hope.

'We don't mind, Joe, do we, Mia?' said Helen, helpfully. Mia shook her head.

'Well, thanks, but I notice you're not doing the same,' Joe pointed out.

'No, personally, I just couldn't. That's why I don't do PE,' said Helen.

'One of the reasons,' said Iz. 'That, and you just don't like it.'

Helen grinned at him. 'Yeah, well, that too.'

Joe said indignantly, 'What? You get off PE just because you don't like getting changed in front of people? Neither do I, but I have to do it.' Joe had been singled out on first sight by Mr Evans as a potential for the rugby team. But Joe had known that he was fat, and no good at sport, and therefore could not be good at rugby. And so, determinedly, he wasn't. He added, disgruntled: 'Couldn't they just let you get changed in private? We should have cubicles, anyway.'

'Yes, why don't we? It's not just that though, I don't want to wear the kit. It shows all your body,' muttered Helen.

Joe knew how she felt, he thought, but he wasn't *that* bad about it. And she wasn't huge and fat. But there. Women. They could be so funny about these things. He said sympathetically:

'Well, they should let you do it in track gear. All of us, for that matter.'

He noticed that, much as Helen didn't want to change in front of everyone else, she was checking over the bare-chested figures around the fire with interest.

Helen thought she was being discreet. She scanned the men briefly with her eyes, intermittently gazing back into the fire.

Chris was quite broad-shouldered, with a man's chest, she thought, fairly good legs, but not really her type somehow. Iz was still rather boyish in build, but had wiry muscles when he moved. Her eyes flicked casually on to Johan, sitting nearest to her. He'd obviously kept a T-shirt on in Australia, then. The skin was dead white against the tan of his neck. Again, she felt a stab of recognition. Warning. Sorrow. Faces, images of people she had known – friends of her mum's, friends of her older brother, a stepdad – flashed through her mind like a series of snapshots. All dead, or in prison, or God-knew-where. Something – something about Johan reminded her . . . She took her eyes off him in case he should notice and glanced back to the fire near his feet. He had taken his socks off, and Helen saw a pattern of sandals picked out in the white and tan stripes there. The white at the base of his ankles was deadly with a tinge of blue.

She felt his strange, mid-brown eyes looking frankly, knowingly at her. She tried to think of something to say, something to deflect him.

'You said you didn't want to come here,' she challenged, 'but you did. You said they got you back. How? You never answered me earlier because there wasn't time.'

The others looked up, interested.

Johan didn't look at them. He answered Helen.

'It's not that I didn't want to come. Well, I suppose it is, let's be honest. It tends to be a very tiring, dangerous time, as you now know, when they ask you to help out. But I do recognise I have a duty. I did recognise that.'

He spoke awkwardly. They could see he was struggling with something, trying to explain when maybe he hadn't got it quite straight with himself. They knew the feeling and said nothing, letting him find his own way.

But the pause went on, and stretched into a silence, until Helen felt a nudge was needed. He had sounded guilty, she thought, a bit defensive. He needed to feel someone was on his side.

'But *why* do you - did you - feel you had a duty? Do you owe them, or something? It seems a horrible thing to do. You've had to risk your neck here time and time again. For what? To get the skull back? To get a bunch of people through, people you don't even know?'

Johan sighed.

'There aren't many dimension shifters. Quite a few are born, but only a few develop the skill so it can be used, as I said. And it's not for David or Gwyn or even the Professor that I came back. It's because once you get involved in the net-repair business, and you know what's at stake, you can't turn your back and pretend it doesn't exist. Be like you were before you knew. I know,' his voice went very quiet, so that the other listeners almost didn't catch what he said, 'because I tried.'

'What happened? Was that when you wouldn't come?'

'Just before then. I got on with my studies. I tried to – be normal. The trouble was, I was a fully-fledged, trained dimension shifter by then. I'd worked with the Professor and David and Gwyn on some very – demanding – assignments. It takes it out of you. But under those conditions, at least the power has a use. You control it carefully, you don't let it control you. Once you've slipped into a dimension, it seems to keep a channel open to you for a while after you've left it. It almost calls you back. Especially if it needs you. When you have control, you can choose to ignore the signal. If you visit lots of dimensions, you must learn to switch them off, or you'd be overrun with signals, demands. Like a computer trying to keep lots of programs open at the same time.'

The fire hissed, spluttered. He glanced into it.

'People who don't know what they've got, who don't let it die or flatten it down; it sends them stark staring crazy. There are some terrible, nightmare realities out there. You can slip into them, just like that. Once in, you have to learn detatchment. You have to keep a hold of your own self. It can be hard.'

'But you said you were trained. Doesn't that mean you can stop it, if you don't like it?' asked Helen.

'It seems to be easier to do that when you're on an assignment. When you're not – well, I think it's like getting a working sheepdog and locking it up in a high-rise flat, trying to take it out for a walk on a lead twice a day. That's how I felt. Noises get to you, without the shepherd's whistle. You want to herd all the wrong things, because there aren't any sheep. People,' he said suddenly, 'people have lots of nets running all through them, holding them together. Can you understand that?'

Helen nodded, doubtfully. She remembered what he'd said about the circulation, lymphatic systems. She saw the diagrams of the skinless human body from her Science books. Was that what he meant?

Iz, listening from the other side, noticed his trainers steaming and wondered if in fact they were starting to smoke. He wanted to move them, but dared not in case Johan stopped talking. He felt as if the man had forgotten they were there.

Johan was leaning forward now, fixing Helen with his steady eyes.

'Sometimes part of one of the nets gets damaged, broken. You can repair it; it takes a long time, but then the repair is good. The right rope, it can even be stronger than before.' He paused. 'But I cheated.'

He looked away and stared back into the fire. Helen was lost. People – rope? She waited.

Johan turned back to her. He spoke as if he had to say it all quickly, or he wouldn't say it at all.

'I used a cheap repair. Quick. But it sets hard. It's hard, so it seems strong. But it is like glass. Soon your whole net is like glass. Shiny, hard, strong, cuts people who try to break it.' He stared at her intently as he spoke, then his voice tailed off to almost a whisper: 'But it's very, very fragile.'

He paused. Then, voice low, he continued without emotion:

'So I was ill. So I couldn't come. I got better. I wanted nothing more to do with all this. I went to Australia. Far away. Lots of sheep.'

Helen didn't understand. Not what he meant; she thought she'd got that. She just didn't understand *how* she understood. She had been listening to him wittering on like a madman about people and rope and nets and being made of glass and part of her, the normal, everyday part, didn't have a clue what he was on about; but somewhere else, in some other part of her, she understood. It went with the things about him she'd recognised: the deathly white parts of him, the twitchy shrug of his shoulder, the way his voice seemed to slip and change, the oldness in his eyes. She didn't want to recognise it. She didn't want to look at him. She put her head down and looked at her knees.

'Ah,' he said sadly, 'you do get it, then.'

Iz, sitting silently on the other side of the fire, felt like screaming in frustration. What was Johan talking about? How did Helen get it, and he didn't? But still he dared not speak. He risked a glance sideways at Joe, who was deep in thought. He looked to his other side. Chris looked back at him, and made a slight face of bewilderment. Iz couldn't bear it. He had to ask.

'Johan, I don't know what you mean. About the net and the repair. You said you were ill?'

Johan looked at him warily, but seemed unwilling to speak.

'Johan talks in riddles because it's too hard to say it straight out. It's his business if he doesn't want everyone to know. But – think of it like a breakdown, Iz. The net which makes you is everything you are, everything that's happened to you. What if it tears apart? And Johan tried to fix it in a stupid way. That's all I think he means.' Helen sat up. Her feet had been starting to scorch. Still she didn't look at Johan.

Helen sounds tired, disappointed, thought Iz. I wonder why?

Johan heard it too. He pulled his knees up, rested his forearms on them and rubbed his chin on his shoulder awkwardly before resting it on one of his wrists.

'You – er, you know, you've met, er, other people like me?' he said, nervously.

Helen looked at him. 'No one like you, Johan. But if you mean – people with similar problems, then yes. Some. Enough.'

'And they were – um . . .'

'Liars. Cheats. Robbers. Selfish. Childish. No good.' Helen spat out the words, one by one.

Johan made a little noise like 'Mm,' and looked harder into the fire.

At last, Helen turned to stare at him.

'But kind. And funny. And different. And full of life. And clever,' she added unexpectedly. Johan looked up again in disbelief.

'I can't say I'll ever *really* understand it, Johan,' Helen continued. 'But I do know that lots of people try to get round their problems, develop stupid habits to avoid the real issues. Maybe not the one you tried. But I used to. Mine seems even more stupid than yours – I didn't even understand it myself.'

'What was your stupid habit, then, Helen?' Joe put in suddenly. 'You bite your nails, like me, don't you?'

'A bit more than that,' said Helen, looking away. 'I don't really want to talk about it, yet.'

'I know,' said Johan, and his eyes flickered to the damp, steaming arms of her long-sleeved T-shirt.

Helen flashed a look at him, then pulled her legs round and tried to make herself comfortable again.

In the silence that followed, Chris lay down flat on his back and put his hands behind his head, looking up at the natural rock ceiling.

'I tell you something,' he said. 'I'm not hungry. Are you? Or thirsty. Odd.'

The others agreed.

'Just as well,' said Joe, 'as I don't think we get rations. I'm not honestly hungry, but I do like to snack a bit. I wish you hadn't mentioned it, Chris.'

'Like to snack a *bit*? I'd say so, mate,' laughed Iz, rolling out of the way of a kick from his friend.

'When everyone feels dry enough, we'll move on,' said Johan. 'We needed this rest, but—'

'You never know how much time you have, here,' interrupted Iz, mimicking Johan's voice.

The others had stood up now and were looking restless, glancing at the walls, checking for change.

Chris, however, was frowning slightly.

'There is one more thing, Johan,' he said. 'You talk as if you don't know why we're here. We do seem a – a pretty strange sort of group. I can't help feeling there's been a bit of a mistake.'

'What?' said Helen, with a slight edge to her voice. 'That we weren't meant to fall into this?'

'Well, um, maybe. But I was thinking of me, actually. I mean, I really don't fit.'

Helen stared at him.

'Oh, I see. You think there's something we all have in common as a group, and you don't share it. What would that be, hey, Chris? You're super smart, and we're all dimwits, spoons, weirdos, is that right?' Her voice had grown louder as she spoke, so that she ended up almost shouting.

'Steady up there, Helen, who are you calling a dimwit?' said Iz, moving in between her and Chris. 'Weirdo, maybe. But I take pride in my brilliant IQ scores. It's one of the things that really ticks off the teachers. Yours aren't too bad, either, I happen to know.'

'How the hell would you know? That's rubbish. I'm in second or bottom set—'

'Ah, but I do know. They shouldn't lock students in offices with everyone's files in, should they?'

'They didn't! They're not allowed to lock you anywhere.'

'Well, all right, they didn't lock the door. But they left me in there for ages on my own, to wait for my mum to pick me up when I was excluded.'

Helen looked dumbfounded.

'I'm sorry, Chris, but your idea doesn't hold water,' said

Johan. 'When I heard that the dimension shift didn't happen until you walked into the room, I knew that it was important that you were there too. The others couldn't go without you.'

'Why the hell did you come into the room in the first place, Chris, no offence?' Iz asked, just before Joe did.

'I went back to get my clipboard, remember, and then I couldn't find my group and I saw Helen and Mia going through this door, so I thought Johan was leading you round and would tell me where to find Gwyn's lot,' Chris said ruefully.

'Why did you have to go back for your clipboard? Why didn't you bring it like everyone else that morning?' asked Johan.

'Yeah, Chris, yeah? Why?' teased Iz.

'Um – I don't know,' Chris confessed. 'I knew I picked it up in my bedroom. I remembered that, when I thought back. But then I didn't seem to have it once I was down at breakfast. I thought I must have put it down in the bathroom or something.'

'Is it like you to forget something?'

'Not really. I'm not too bad, as a rule. I was a bit surprised.'

'Did you find it?'

'Yes, it was just on the bedside table in my room after all. I must have put it down for a moment.'

Johan shrugged. 'Well, whatever happened, Chris, it was meant to be. If the clipboard hadn't ended up there instead of in your hands, you would have missed this exciting trip.'

Chris frowned and thought for a moment.

'Are you saying – are you saying, someone did that? Messed about with my clipboard like that? To make me end up—'

'In the right place at the right time,' Johan said smoothly.

He's winding up Chris on purpose, thought Iz. I think he knew darned well what Chris meant when he said he didn't belong with us. Good on you, Johan.

Joe smiled at him as they set off behind Johan, and Iz knew he'd picked up on the same thing. Helen trotted up behind him.

'What were my scores, Iz? And why were you looking at *my* file, anyway?'

'I looked at everyone's file. I had loads of time. Some other teacher was supposed to come and guard me, but they never turned up. Yours were pretty good. I wouldn't have known, but they were on a list for the whole year as well, and they were circled as high. You did particularly well at, er, verbal something and something gross . . . gross verbal, probably, which means you're really good at swearing . . .'

He ducked, just in time, as Helen swung for him. Joe dived out of the way, giggling. Even Johan was smiling.

'I think Iz meant verbal reasoning, which is very good, and the other one is probably something like gross and fine motor skills, but I'm only guessing.'

'Nah, Helen doesn't know anything about cars, do you, Helen?' said Iz, trotting backwards in front of her, deftly avoiding the swats from her hands.

'That's big movements, and very careful fiddly movements, like – I don't know, putting together a tiny fuse board. Embroidery,' Johan threw back helpfully over his shoulder.

'I didn't think I was any good at – well, I suppose I *can*. It's just the patience.'

'Good thing you went up to move the lights after all, Helen,' said Joe. 'You were just the right one for it.'

She smiled at him graciously.

'Thank you, Joe.'

'Shame you nearly killed me first by swinging the lever the wrong way and making all the beasts rush right over to us, but besides that . . .'

Johan gave up his helpful interventions, and Chris and Mia kept close to him to avoid becoming entangled in the debate.

After somebody punched too hard, and a brief argument about whether one should apologise for something if it wasn't intended, and anyway, there was a hint that the victim was making a fuss about nothing, the scuffling and yelping stopped and was replaced by a rather bruised silence.

As they rounded a slight bend, they were surprised to see the tunnel ended not in the archway to a cave they had expected, but in a rather plain white door. It was a very solid-looking door, on the square side of rectangular, apparently made not of wood but perhaps of metal, with a very small round disc for a handle. Like a door at a bank or something, thought Helen.

All of them felt it was some kind of security door. Would they be able to open it? Iz looked at Johan, wondering if he had a key or a code. To his surprise, Johan simply tried the strange handle, and the door swung inwards easily, with a heavy creak.

They peered in.

Instead of a cave, they were looking into a large room, very plain but with smooth white plastered walls and a wooden floor. They looked up and saw a proper ceiling, with a real, single light bulb hanging from the middle on a slightly dirty piece of white flex.

'I don't like this,' said Helen.

'I know what you mean,' said Chris. 'I like to see another door out.'

'But the caves were like that,' said Iz, 'and a new archway always appears. At least I can't see any beasties in here. And it is a room, not a cave.'

'True,' said Joe. 'Mind you, I wouldn't trust it. Not here.'

'We must go in, however,' said Johan, apologetically. 'No other option.'

'Mouse,' said Mia, for no apparent reason, and walked first into the room, scouting around the floor with odd little movements of her eyes.

The others looked around dubiously.

'Did you really see a mouse, Mia?' said Joe. 'I wonder what it's doing down here? Do you see it now?'

Mia glanced around again, shook her head and shrugged.

'Where could it go?' Iz asked, watching Johan carefully. He noticed that Johan had a keen, sharp look about him. He was staring around, listening, almost sniffing.

'Hmm?' said Johan, not really listening to him.

Joe was wandering around the floor of the room, looking down.

'There's big enough gaps in the floorboards here, Iz. Not so much gaps as squares cut through the planks for accessing electrics, or something.'

'Joe! Get back off there! Come over here, now!' said Johan urgently.

Joe leapt from the far end of the room and to Johan's side.

They were all staring at their guide in surprise. He had almost shouted. They'd never heard Johan shout.

'Never trust a floor that's cut like that,' said Johan, sounding calmer. 'It's sound here, where we're standing, see. Don't worry about Mia's mouse. It won't do any harm.' Johan looked about him, this way and that and then up at the ceiling. 'I just wonder if—'

They didn't have a chance to hear what Johan wondered. At that moment, there was a deafening crash, and the ceiling at the far end, where Joe had been only a few seconds before, splintered into pieces and was flung to the corners of the room. Helen backed up as a fragment landed near her shoe. They cowered around Johan.

Helen managed to find breath to speak at last.

'What is it? What the heck . . . !'

Two massive boulders had rolled and thudded to a rest on the floor in front of them. They waited for the dust to settle.

'Crikey, Johan, I don't think it was the cut floor you needed to warn Joe about,' said Iz. 'The Class A rocks dropping through the Bog Standard ceiling was more the thing to look out for. Still, you got the danger zone right.'

Joe was staring horrified at the boulders. Iz had started to move towards them. He glanced up at the ceiling.

'Look!' he called to the others, 'The sky! Lovely, lovely sky!'

The others looked up at the ruined half of the ceiling. They could see the dark sky, the odd cloud, a flicker of a star here and there. There was a faint movement of air on their cheeks, gently lifting a stray hair, bringing the wild scent of night.

'There are circles on these.'

Iz's voice, puzzled and almost indignant, brought their eyes down from the heavens.

'Iz, I don't think you should walk on that floor,' said Johan sharply.

'I tell you, Johan, it's held up under these flipping things dropping on it, hasn't it? There are circles on the rocks. Carved or something. Quite a few.' Iz looked more closely. 'In fact, I think the rocks are carved. The edges are rather nice – almost bevelled, they look. And the circles – they're spaced dead even.'

Chris, in spite of himself, picked his way cautiously across the floor and looked at the boulders with Iz.

'He's right, you know,' he called back to Johan, 'I can't believe these are natural. It's like they're designed. They're sort of rounded-off cubes. Or cubed-off circles. A bit like—'

'GET OVER HERE NOW!' Johan almost screamed.

Before Iz and Chris could make any response, the boulders suddenly shifted, crunching together, and flew in the air.

As the boys stared, unable to believe what their eyes were seeing, the boulders fell again, crashing on to the floor with such force that the group huddled at the end of the room staggered slightly at the vibration. Chris was taken off his feet and landed face down on the floor; the boulder which had slammed into the ground behind him bounced, skimmed his body, narrowly missed his head and ricocheted off the wall, leaving a large dent, and came to rest in front of his face.

Iz luckily dived the right way as the second boulder landed near him, so that he and the missile ended up travelling in opposite directions. He skidded on his knees and ended up in front of the terrified group huddled around Johan.

The rumbling and shaking stopped. There was a final grinding from one of the boulders as it toppled to its resting place; fragments of plaster and clouds of dust settled slowly.

Iz, still on his knees, looked up at Johan. His eyes shone out amidst the grime on his face.

'Oops,' he said.

Chris was raising himself up on to all fours. They could see he wasn't trapped under a boulder, but they weren't sure if he had been hit. Iz pulled himself upright and started towards him.

'Wait, Iz,' said Johan. 'Listen, this time, at least.'

He spoke quietly, but Iz realised he had a point. He'd tried to tell them before. Iz stopped.

'Chris, are you hurt?' called Johan.

Chris shook his head, wiped his face with one hand, and called back, 'Don't think so,' in a shaky voice.

'Then get on your feet and get over here NOW!' shouted Johan.

Chris stood up very slowly.

'You heard what he said. Get a bloody move on!' shouted Helen. 'You stay there and you won't be all right for long, mate.'

Chris, who had been frozen with fear, now sprang into action, too scared to stay where he was.

'Did they trigger a booby trap or something, Johan?' asked Joe.

'No, it wasn't their fault,' said Johan. 'It was going to happen anyway.'

Chris had reached them. He looked very pale and his hands shook as he swept dust from his jeans.

'What in God's name happened then? How did the rocks jump up in the air again?'

'It wasn't an earthquake,' said Iz quickly, 'because the ground didn't shake before it happened. It only shook when the rocks fell back down again.'

'They're not rocks,' said Johan, 'they're dice.'

'They're dice?' Iz was aghast. 'Then who the – who's throwing them? They should be more bloody careful.'

'No one's throwing them. They are simply running through a series of hypothetical outcomes. You happened to be in the way.'

'So long as we might only have been hypothetically injured or killed,' said Chris, outraged. 'What do you mean, no one's throwing them? They are leaping about somehow. Talking of which – are they going to do it again?'

At that moment there was a scraping sound as the huge dice rolled themselves from their resting places and launched weightily into the air. Everyone backed away to the farthest wall and put their hands over their ears.

Again, there was a crashing and splintering. Helen closed her eyes, waiting for the sharp blow on the head, the thud, the crushing weight on her legs, perhaps. Then the thumping stopped, and she dared to look around, and found everyone else was doing the same. Somehow the floor, though scarred, remained intact. One of the boulders had rolled very close to them before coming to rest.

'I was going to say, yes,' said Johan, checking that everyone was unhurt, 'I think they are going to do it a few times, unfortunately. And I expect we should be preparing for something; there will be a connection with getting out of here. I just don't see what it is. Until it ends' – at that moment they heard the dreadful sound of the boulders picking themselves up again – 'just stick together and keep your heads down.'

He shouted the last part over the boom of falling rock. This time, the boulders hit each other and bounced apart. One of the boulders hit the wall just above their heads, fired back again and ended up at rest at the other end of the room.

In the pause, Helen shuffled over to Mia, who was curled up into a small ball with her hands over her ears, rocking. Helen wrapped her arms around Mia as tightly as she could. The faint sounds of muffled humming reached her ears.

'This just isn't fair,' Helen called to Johan. 'Mia isn't made for this.' She was almost tearful. Joe swung across the floor on his fists sideways, like an ape. He too wrapped his arms around Mia. He wasn't sure whether he was doing it for Mia, or for Helen.

They stayed that way as the rocks leapt up, crashed down, fired around them, for what seemed like an age. Chris, Iz and Johan tried to stay in a bunch nearby, but every so often had to split to dodge an approaching die. After several near misses, Iz glanced across at the huddle around Mia.

'Joe! Helen! You lot aren't safe keeping still. Stay there long enough and one's going to hit you.'

'Interesting theory of randomness, Iz, but not necessarily correct,' said Johan.

At that moment the dice, which had risen and hovered for

a moment behind their backs as they spoke, crashed to the ground, and one fired straight at the three gripped together.

Joe saw it coming and dived one way, rolling Mia with him; Helen felt them torn from her hands and leapt the other way, in the nick of time. The die hurtled through the middle, bounced off the wall and shot back again to the far end of the room.

'And a fine theory, Iz, which I think we'll follow from now on,' said Johan, the first to recover.

'This may seem like a silly question, Johan, but we couldn't just go out the door again, could we?' said Iz, half-crawling towards him.

Johan, who was standing near the door, reached out and opened it. There was nothing but a blur on the other side.

'I thought so,' said Iz. 'Any idea yet of how we get through this?'

'I have a sort of an idea,' said Johan. 'I don't think the blur is going to start pushing us until the dice have stopped. But there's something bad about the floor. We may have to make decisions quickly. Has anyone been keeping the score?'

'The score? What the hell are you talking about? Boulders five, us zero?'

'I told you, they're not boulders,' Johan said patiently. 'They're dice. And the throws are each giving a score. We haven't been counting. It might be important.'

Iz whistled and beckoned to Chris.

As the boulders crashed down once more, Chris darted out of their path and managed to reach Iz and Johan in a series of leaps.

'What?' he gasped, out of breath.

'You're good at Maths, aren't you?'

'Well, I—'

'What set are you in?'

'Top set. And some of us do special extension work.' Chris put his head down modestly.

'Do you do that – the extension work?' asked Iz, his tone urgent.

'Well, yes.'

'We'll need you for this one, maybe. Johan here says the dice are making a score every time they fall. We haven't been noticing what they land on; have you?'

'It hasn't been uppermost in my mind.'

'We'd have a job seeing, most of the time. The face that's uppermost, anyway,' said Iz.

'But you probably *have* noticed. I mean, you don't think you have, but your eyes have probably seen which face is pointing where and so on, so you *could*, in theory, work out which number was uppermost,' said Johan calmly. 'From your knowledge of dice, I mean.'

'What the flip are you on about, Johan?'

Johan sighed. 'If you were to use the screen, I bet it would tell you all the throws so far. With *all* of your inputs.'

Iz slapped his forehead. 'Screen! Great idea! Don't know what you're on about, but I like the screen. I'll get the others.'

As the dice crashed around the room for what seemed like the umpteenth time, Iz managed to beckon the others over.

'Right,' he explained, 'Johan says the screen is the thing, and we should have thought of it already.'

'It was hard to think of anything with *that* going on,' said Helen.

'Ready, everyone? Try not to be distracted by all the thumps and crashes. Let's get a move on while they're having a rest.'

'That might have been the last one,' said Johan. 'It has to stop sometime.'

'Good,' said Mia suddenly. Johan smiled at her.

'In a way, Mia. But I think when they stop, we have then only a short time to act.'

'So let's get on,' said Helen. 'Everyone think.'

The screen appeared so quickly this time that they all looked at each other in surprise, not quite sure who had been responsible for its speed.

'Getting good at this,' said Iz, rubbing his hands together. 'Now – ah – what have we had thrown then? Aha!'

A table appeared on the screen.

'There we go. Now, Chris, take a look, man. We're relying on you.'

Chris leant in. 'Yep, OK. It's just a normal frequency table. Looks like something to do with probability, I'd say.'

They all stared at it.

Joe said, 'Oh, I know. We did this with flipping a coin, I think, once. Is that the same thing, Chris? Only we put in H or T for Heads or Tails.'

'Yeah, that's it.'

'I didn't mind that too much,' said Joe, 'though I don't like Maths because I'm no good at it.'

'It can't help not being able to read the questions, mate,' said Iz sympathetically, 'because you aren't that bad at Maths otherwise. You always work out the money when we go to the shop or something. You were always better than me at that.'

'Dimension edges closing fast,' said Johan suddenly.

All of them except for Mia looked behind at the wall and door. It had faded into the familiar blur.

Mia said clearly, 'Mouse.'

Helen looked round, irritated. She didn't much like mice, they made her jump. It was all very well, Mia saying off-the-wall things, but this wasn't the time. But – *was* that a mouse she saw scuttling over the floor just then?

'Mia's right,' Helen said. 'Mind you, I think it was bigger than a mouse. God, I hope it wasn't a rat. It looked – do you know something?' she said, her voice changing abruptly, 'I do believe there are numbers on the floor. I never noticed them before. Look! I swear I can see a six.'

They followed her finger, pointing.

'There's an eight – and a three – and another . . .'

The figures were only visible as shiny shapes contrasting with the dusty matt of the battered floorboards.

'They must have some sort of coating,' said Chris, 'so we didn't see them before all the dust fell. It seems to stick to where the numbers aren't.'

'Thank God the dice have stopped,' said Helen.

Iz addressed the screen. 'We've got a table of numbers here, and numbers on the floor – but not in the same order, I notice – and we have a blur right behind us. What the heck is going to happen as we move ahead across the floor?'

The screen flashed. It pushed the table of numbers to the top right-hand side. It showed what they took to be the floor in front of them, with numbers appearing in squares. They checked, looked back to the screen.

'That's the floor layout all right,' said Helen cautiously. 'What are the squares though?'

'That's where the wood was cut!' said Joe, inspired. 'It's like traps you cut for plumbing and electric access, I said.'

'Traps?' said Mia.

They watched as the familiar white circles moved towards the squares. As a circle moved over a square, the square seemed to disappear along with the white circle, leaving behind a black hole.

'I don't like the look of that,' Iz muttered.

'Right, there'll be an order – ow!' Helen banged suddenly into Chris, who sidestepped, just missing Johan.

'Move in, everyone. The edges are coming this way – and quickly,' said Johan.

They shuffled hurriedly to the edge of the floor area, which had numbers etched upon it. Helen looked affronted at the blur as it gained the ground they'd just left, and rubbed her arm.

They stared into the screen again.

'I was saying, there will be an order you have to tread on the squares, maybe,' said Helen.

'I'm not so sure. I don't think I want to tread on any of them,' said Joe. 'I think they are going to drop you straight away, if you tread on the wrong one. It's a pity we can't check out every scenario possibility.'

'That would take too long,' said Johan, 'we're nearly out of time now. But I do think you're right, Joe. I think there's perhaps only one safe square. Last chance to try the screen. Either that or, if our theory is correct, you've only a' – he counted rapidly – 'one in seven chance of hitting the right square.'

Chris was staring from the table of numbers at the top of the screen back to the drawing of the floor layout.

'Same numbers appear in the floor layout, it's just they aren't repeated. OK,' he said, wiping sweat from his upper lip. 'It's all very well being good at Maths. But I'm not really seeing a question here.'

'To hell with the Maths,' said Helen. 'Which is the safe square?'

With a little 'ping', the screen displayed the words: 'most frequent total'.

Without warning, Johan pulled them into a wobbling line at the edge of the cut squares. They could now make the squares out clearly. Each one was very large. If it fell away, there didn't seem to be a possibility of grabbing the edges.

It was now impossible for them all to see the screen, as they could no longer stand in a semi circle. The blur seemed to be advancing even now. The screen hovered just in front of Chris and Joe.

Joe didn't really understand the table, but the words 'most frequent' buzzed in his head. He saw the pattern of numbers; there was no time to count.

Helen and Iz screamed and staggered as the blur hit them. Johan wobbled and shouted: 'Don't touch the squares!' All of them teetered for a moment; then Joe shouted, in a voice quite unlike his own: 'NINE!' and leapt.

With nowhere else to go, the others were only a fraction behind him. As each landed, they grabbed the next person to arrive, desperate not to be knocked off the square.

Gripping tightly to each other, they saw the blur advance. It paused for a moment; then there was a great creaking, and with an eardrum-bursting sound of crushing metal, every square around them simply dropped away. Helen, her fingers twisting tight into T-shirts either side of her, looked down into a black hole of nothingness which had opened just by her left foot, and instinctively dragged it further in. The group squeezed together more tightly in the centre of their square. Surrounded by yawning dark chasms, they felt precarious, as if perched on a rock at sea, and everyone crouched slightly. And then, quite without warning, their feet were being pushed up to meet them; air pressed heavy on their backs, and they folded their knees; they had the horrid sensation of going up in a lift too quickly. Because they were all facing the centre of the square no one understood what was happening. Then, as the floor of the room with its black holes dropped away below them, they realised. The wooden section of floor on which they were standing, with its imprinted number nine beneath their feet, had been fired like an ejector seat into the night sky.

CHAPTER FOURTEEN

The wind bit into their faces and made their eyes stream. They heard nothing but a high-pitched whine singing through their bodies; they were being forced up through air which pressed hard down on their heads, made their knees collapse with the weight of it. They squatted on the board, every hand grabbing on to either a piece of someone else, or the wood on which they flew, fingers digging deep between the boards for some kind of hold. Splinters ran deep; blood was drawn by desperate nails. Lungs trapped and squeezed painfully in his chest, Joe felt none of it. He just wanted to get a breath, or have this over with quickly and die now.

Iz tried to open his eyes but could not see through the blinding tears. He curled his head down and tried again. The wind forced his hair flat down either side of his head; it felt like it was being torn out by the roots. Still, when he tried to open his eyes this time, he could see. It was dark, night apparently, like when they had found themselves beside the brook. But, again, there was enough light by which to see the wooden flooring, slightly varnished, in front of his bent knees. He risked a look sideways and saw Johan's leg, a flap of pale denim battered about in the wind. Carefully flicking his eyes in the other direction without lifting his head, he saw Joe's knee near his own. At the very corner of his vision, beyond Joe, he thought he could make out Chris's T-shirt. He tried to look in front of him, but when he tilted his head up slightly, the wind smacked his hair over his eyes and he could not catch a breath. Before it did so, however, he just caught a glimpse of two other heads beneath waterfalls of hair, and knew the girls were still with them.

Helen had heard screaming from several directions when the terrifying launch had started, but was surprised to find herself silent. Shock, for one thing, she thought, and then later, it was almost impossible to grab enough air to breathe, let alone scream. Part of her felt that they must have made a mistake, picked the wrong number. They were surely going to die. But then, as the journey upward started to slow and the whining roar of the air pressure died, she thought of the gaping black chasms left by the other numbers and realised they had made the best choice. As the terrible ascent slowed more noticeably, Helen started to feel little seeds of hope somewhere deep inside. A moment more, and she could lift her head.

She could just about see, now, though her long hair lashed around her face, flicking her eyes painfully every now and then, getting in her mouth. Her plan had been to look down, but the first thing she saw was the person directly opposite her, and that was Iz.

Iz raised his chin, let go of Johan's shoulder for a moment to brush his dark hair out of his eyes, then blinked a few times and looked back straight at her. She could see him clearly in the moonlight; his dog eyes had a steady glitter to them.

He opened his mouth and tried to shout something to her. She thought she could just make out something about his enjoying it. She shook her head at him. She dared not move, although they seemed to be slowing almost every second now.

He shuffled slightly closer to her, still crouched, still keeping a hand on Johan and Joe. She lowered her head next to his.

'I said, I like it,' shouted Iz.

'You would,' said Helen, wondering if this would be the last conversation they would ever have. Surely the dreadful fall would begin soon, unless Johan was going to come up with something.

'No, not *this*,' Iz shouted, 'your hair. That wild look. It suits you.'

It cost him enormous effort to shout. Helen stared at him in disbelief, then managed to roll her eyes up at him. Why not? What better way to go than with a bit of a laugh, for God's sake? She gathered her breath.

'We're slowing. There might be – plan. Before – fall. Johan.'

Iz heard her all right, but looked doubtfully at her. What about Johan?

'Kick him – Johan,' Helen managed to shout, exasperation making her grab breath where she had thought there was none.

Iz shook Johan's shoulder. Johan turned his head sideways towards Iz. His eyes looked quite calm.

'Plan?' shouted Iz. 'This normal?'

Johan screwed his face up, whether in a frown or smile, Iz couldn't be sure.

'Get heads to the middle. All.'

Iz shuffled forward again to Helen and passed the message on. Then he backed up and tapped and pulled Joe to get his attention.

Joe, trapped in a hell of suffocation, tried to suck in a lungful of precious air, but found he couldn't.

Iz watched him worriedly, as he gaped like a fish out of water. Suddenly something clicked inside Joe's head, and he realised he had not let out the breath which was clamped inside him. He exhaled with a great rushing sound, and sucked air back in greedily.

Iz had sat with Joe in a paramedic car once. He shouted: 'Steady mate, bit slower. Slow and deep,' and he carried on shouting until Joe nodded furiously to show he'd understood, and started to breathe more easily. With Joe looking better, Iz managed to indicate a move towards the centre of the board. Chris, already alerted by all the movement, looked across Joe at Iz and nodded to show he understood. He looked slightly sick, pale against the backdrop of the dark sky, but he had a determined tilt to his jaw. Helen had already persuaded Mia towards the middle by dint of a little pull on her arm and a smile through gritted teeth.

Mia looked at her. Why is she smiling, and in such an odd way? she thought. Stuck on a piece of floor, in the dark, thousands of metres in the air, and people will still make the strangest faces. This is one bit of human etiquette they didn't cover in social skills training, she thought, which emotion one should express or suppress in a situation like this. Strangely enough, Mia found herself smiling at her own thoughts. Helen, on seeing the smile, started to grin back. Mia sensed that perhaps they didn't think so very differently. She shunted forwards awkwardly, gripping between the boards as best she could with her fingers.

They were now mostly on all fours, occasionally reaching out a hand or arm to a friend to steady themselves. Heads together in the centre of the square of wood, Iz felt that if anyone could see them from a plane, they would look like some bizarre aerial acrobatic team preparing for a stunt.

'It's not as bad as it seems,' Johan shouted.

'You've got six pocket parachutes,' Iz tried.

'Not exactly. Don't need them. Now . . .'

Johan paused, a watchful look on his face. They had stopped climbing; their hair, clothes, and insides, from being rammed downwards, suddenly flew up in the air. For a moment, they felt as if their whole bodies were floating just a hairsbreadth above the boards. Then gravity took over again and they regained a sense of weight and stability.

'OK,' Johan began again, 'we've levelled out. We only have to glide down. Now, I don't want any of you to panic. Do you promise me that?'

They nodded solemnly.

'Listen carefully. If you do not panic, you will be fine. If you do panic, I can do nothing to help you, nor can anyone else, and I'm afraid you will almost certainly die. Are you still listening?' Johan had lowered his voice. There was no need to shout, now that the screaming air pressure had stopped. Having felt the bitter cold of the streaming air current on her skin, Helen realised she was now almost warm. She tingled as if she had come out of the sea. She felt very alive. She wanted to stay that way, to enjoy it. She looked at Johan and nodded again.

He seemed to prepare his mouth before he spoke. Then he said clearly: 'In this environment, you can all fly.'

They looked back at him cautiously. Thoughts flew. Something to say to make the poor children's last moments less terrifying. The words of a madman. A possible truth. There's bound to be a catch.

Johan waited. He saw their eyes, the thoughts go inwards, back outwards to him, come to some resolution. He repeated:

'In this environment ONLY, you can all fly. Now, a bird can fly. But if it doesn't know it, if it's never done it before, well, it isn't going to be very good. But good enough. Just to glide down.'

Iz still eyed him narrowly. He trusted very few people, and particularly few adults, but he liked the idea. He had always wanted to fly, and he thought he wouldn't be half bad.

'We won't be able to stay together on this board, but I imagine you'll get a part each. You'll still have something to surf on. Ideal for first-timers. But please remember – if you do lose your board, you can still make it down alive.' Johan spoke simply, his words ringing out on the night air. They saw his figure, bathed in moonlight which sucked the colour from everything it touched; it made him seem ageless. 'It won't be gravity which kills you – it will be your own mind.'

They were scared, impressed with the words. Except for Iz. He gave a little cough.

'Be honest, Johan,' he said. 'Even if you lose it and go head-first like a lead budgie without wings and very heavy cannonballs tied to its legs, it will still be gravity that kills you. In the end.'

Chris managed a shaky grin. 'You know he's right,' he called to Johan, who rolled his eyes.

'You get my point, though, all of you? Good. Because when this board levels off, which is what is happening now, that's when it breaks up. We need to get ready. All link arms over shoulders and stand.'

As they tried to scramble to their feet, they felt a rising sense of panic. It was all very well in theory. But not holding on and standing up? That seemed truly terrifying. Not for the first time, they wished they were somewhere else.

Helen put an arm behind Mia's neck and over her far shoulder and did the same with Johan. As she tried to stand up straight, she found her knees strangely creaky and weak. At a certain point they seemed unable to straighten any more. As the whole group stood slowly, linked, rising together, they found the same thing. They stood, wobbling uncertainly, legs slightly bent. The board kept smooth and level, and the wind was steady and no longer freezing. Johan, taller than all of them, found himself uncomfortably stooped, weighed down by Helen and Iz's arms around his neck.

'Now, listen, we haven't long for you to get used to this. Look down at the board. See the diagonal lines? Shove your foot over a bit, Joe, would you? Yes, there, you can see them. The board will divide along that, giving five good arrows, or triangles you'd call them, in a moment. Each of you make sure you are on a board. Sorry, Iz, I have to crowd you on yours for a moment longer. I'll try not to unbalance you.'

Iz looked at him, baffled. 'But if there's only five triangles – what are *you* going to do, Johan?'

'I told you, you don't really need the boards in this dimension. I've managed without plenty of times. But for first-timers, it's scary enough. These give you a feeling of security.'

'Oh yeah, right,' said Helen, next to him, 'very secure.'

'Like a float at the swimming pool,' said Joe, ignoring her, and looking with concentration at Johan.

'That's it, Joe. Or stabilisers on a bike. And often you don't even need them. You don't realise you're managing anyway. I promise you can do this, with or without the boards.'

There was a strange feeling of movement suddenly, which made Helen crouch instinctively, dragging Johan's neck down again. They all felt it, the pulling on their arm muscles.

'The boards are dividing,' shouted Chris, looking down. He had done some skateboarding, and felt suddenly worried for the others; maybe not everyone had that advantage. There must be some last-minute advice that would help.

He looked anxiously at Johan.

'It's a bit like boarding, yeah?'

Johan nodded, trying to pull Helen into a more upright stance.

Chris went on: 'Same things apply? Foot forward, push the nose down, you'll go down, and increase speed. Weight on back foot, let nose lift, you'll go up, slow up.' Chris acted as if he was still talking to Johan, but flashed urgent looks at

Helen and Mia. He didn't want to sound bossy. His voice was cracking under the effort of shouting in the windstream. Iz interrupted.

'Helen, Mia. You listening? And you, Joe? No? Well, flipping listen. There isn't time. Not even for a crash course. But a few basics would help. Keep them in your head.'

'No panic,' said Johan. He carefully disentangled himself from Helen and Iz, and linked them together, backing out of the strange circle and balancing perilously on the back edge of Iz's triangle, which already showed a gap of several centimetres around its inner edges. 'We can start off linked together in a line. You'll feel safer like that for a while.'

'Go on, Chris, what you were saying sounded good,' called Iz encouragingly.

Chris looked at him slightly warily. You never knew when Iz was taking the mickey.

'Keep crouched a little, but that's a bit much, Helen. Remember, standing more upright slows you, which I think we'll all want to do. Feet apart about as wide as your hips. Whoa! Coming apart now. Can you still hear me? We need to get lined up.' Chris felt his section of board drifting backwards as it detached from the group. With Mia and Joe's arms staying linked around the back of his neck, he was nearly pulled off forwards.

They were now floating separately. They saw nothing but darkness between the boards at first; then they caught sight of little wisps of cloud, and a dull suggestion of trees far below in the moonlight.

Iz felt the nose of his board lift. He couldn't think why it was happening; he hadn't moved. He leant far forward and

159

pushed down hard on the nose with his foot, catching it just in time.

'I'm off, I'm off,' he heard Johan's voice behind him. 'Sorry, Iz, I should have got off quicker. Helen, I'll hold your hand now for a bit. We'll be the end of the line. Let Iz go.'

Helen, who had nearly had her arm wrenched out of its socket trying to hang on to Iz when he had suddenly lifted in the air, was happy to do as she was told.

Johan swept forwards, upwards, then seemed to regain control and hang at Helen's side for a moment. He looked like a tethered kite, Iz thought. It obviously wasn't easy, like treading water. Then Helen and Johan whirled away from him as the line straightened out.

Iz glanced at Joe, still gripping his shoulder.

'All right?' he called. To his surprise, Joe turned and nodded with a grin.

'Great!' he shouted back.

Helen was gripping Johan's hand tightly, but it was rather like holding a leaping dog. Still, she'd rather have him there than not at all. She had Mia's shoulder in her other hand, and Mia held hers. Strangely, Mia felt the most steady, her board barely fluctuating.

Chris, between Mia and Joe, had looked first at the small, slender girl on his left, then at the burly figure on his right, and wondered who to worry about most. After the first few moments, he realised that neither was pulling him about. Glancing at Mia's face, he saw its sculptured calmness in the dark, and felt relieved. Joe was shouting something to Iz, and seemed, amazingly, to be smiling.

Johan, his body bent into a curve like a bowstring, swept

up again, and his hand pulled free of Helen's. A second later, and he was back at her side, his hand on her shoulder.

'Easier if I let go, if you're OK, Helen. I'm pulling you off balance. Will you be OK?' he shouted.

Helen felt a little sick, but nodded.

And then Johan was off, somewhere perhaps above her. She tilted her head back to see him, but immediately her board started to climb, and she panicked and pressed the nose back down again by stamping a foot forwards. Now the board dived, and she felt herself yank Mia's shoulder with her hand. Furious with herself, she slid her foot slowly back to a sensible position, and the board levelled off again amidst shouts of distress from the rest of the line.

Mia, back alongside, called: 'Do you feel all right, Helen?'

'Yes, yes, fine, sorry about that,' Helen called back.

Johan swept in front of them, his body horizontal, chest thrust forward, arms outstretched either side of him, legs together, toes pointed, face forward, streamlined, exactly like a bird; nothing like the freefall position Helen had expected. He darted this way and that, tacking side to side, which seemed to be the best way he had of keeping himself airborne at slower speeds. It did look strangely beautiful, Helen thought, though a bit odd somehow in jeans, an old T-shirt and trainers.

Mia was calling to her, she realised suddenly.

'If you are all right, I will let go now then, please,' Mia shouted.

Helen felt a stab of fear, but realised that Mia was being quite reasonable because she, Helen, had insisted that she was fine. Just for a moment, Helen felt like kicking herself for her stupid pride, but she smiled at Mia and nodded, and let go only a moment after Mia released her.

Mia felt Helen's hand slip from her shoulder, and relaxed a little more. It had been far more difficult trying to fly linked together. One person made a mistake and it pulled everyone in the line out of place.

Chris was of the same opinion. He was relieved when Mia let go. He turned to Joe and Iz.

'Joe, shall we try it without holding on? I think it would be easier,' he shouted.

In a moment, they were all separated, Chris moving slightly ahead of Joe, but slowing to keep an eye on him.

Iz felt the pulse and pressure of the air below his board, the dips and bulges of turbulence as solid as those of water, but invisible. The night air prickled against his skin and his scalp, made his hair lift. He saw Johan fly into view again with that strange, sideways swoop, grabbing Iz's elbow for a moment. Iz had to shake him off as he immediately lost balance.

'What?' Iz shouted. He just caught sight of Johan pointing downwards, before he swept away again, in front of the others, like an agitated bird.

Cautiously, Iz managed to speed up enough to draw alongside Joe, who seemed to be enjoying himself. Iz was cautious, sure that if the board tilted too much, it would simply be swept out from under his feet by the air pressure. He wasn't quite sure how he'd kept the board with him even this long.

Slowing the board, he saw Johan's message seemed to have been picked up by the others, who were all repeating his downward gesture at each other.

Landing – maybe easier said than done, thought Iz, looking down. But Johan was right. They had been falling steadily for a while now, and the land was rising up rapidly to meet them. He could make out scrubby trees, maybe bracken, strange shadows creating ripples, and the smooth top of a hill or mound below, clear of trees and flattened; an ideal landing site. If they didn't make an attempt at a controlled descent here, they would soon crash in any case.

He pushed the nose of the board down towards the hilltop. Immediately, the wind speed increased, and tears whipped from his eyes. Joe appeared to one side of him as a dark form, and Iz realised that Johan was just above his shoulder somewhere. He couldn't catch what Johan was shouting, but realised that he was much too fast and would never make the landing. He leant back hard, the nose lifted, and he soared upwards again. He was just pushing his foot back to the nose to compensate for his over-correction when he felt the board, unable to cope with the extreme angle, catch the wind and shoot away from beneath him, flipping over as it went.

Iz felt his feet pedalling in the air uselessly for a moment. Then he started to fall, but was surprised to find that his arms, still out from his sides for balance, seemed to steady him against the wind. It was as if invisible webbing ran from his arms to his body. The air pressure wanted to snap his arms upwards, behind his back, so it was with some effort he kept them spread wide. But he remembered what Johan had said. You didn't need the board anyway.

Johan swept in front of him again. Iz felt he was still falling too fast, despite his best efforts. If he landed like this, he would surely break both legs. He heard Johan shout again as he passed so closely they almost brushed each other: 'Lie forward. Like this.'

Iz let his feet rise up behind him. He kept his arms stiffly outstretched, despite the drag on his muscles, the determined pulling at his clothes by the wind. Almost immediately, his downward movement changed to forwards. A bit like swimming underwater, thought Iz. Now he was banking, swooping, circling after Johan. If you just did it and didn't think about it, it came quite naturally, he found. He realised Johan was guiding him round the top of the strange flattened hill, above its ridged and shadowed flanks, back for another landing attempt.

He wondered for a moment about the others. Then, as he spiralled down behind Johan in a series of fits and starts, he saw figures below him on the moonlit hilltop, and as they swept down closer, he could see they were holding boards, looking up at him. He wanted to shout, 'I'm OK!' He could tell even from here that they were worried.

How to land? He kept an eye on Johan. Both of them were low now, only metres above the ground. He seemed to see in a way he never had before – despite the darkness, despite the rushing speed of their descent, the odd stone or flint and the individual blades of grass seemed to leap out at him from the ground; and was that a scurrying rabbit? He caught a glimpse of Helen, Joe – then they were a blur as he sped past. Johan had turned his arms, Iz could see, so that the backs of his hands were now at right angles to the ground instead of parallel, above it. He was scooping air, swinging his arms back and pushing hard forwards. It was almost as if he were swimming backwards. Iz copied as best he could.

Immediately, his speed slowed and his legs began to fall of their own accord. His arms ached; every muscle screamed. The air felt heavy and thick. Still he fought his speed, circling his arms as fast as he could like a rower, until his feet caught a tussock of grass and he fell, his shoulder smacking hard into the earth, bouncing him once, before he rolled several times over with a speed and violence which shocked him, and came to rest finally in cool, damp grass.

CHAPTER FIFTEEN

Iz lay gasping for a moment, staring up at the starry sky, wallowing in the relief of feeling his own weight pressing his back, the backs of his legs, his heels, his shoulders, the back of his skull, down into the solid earth of a great hill. He saw his fellow travellers' anxious faces appear above him, but he didn't care. He had to lie here for a moment and sweep his arms and legs, lovingly, through the realness of the damp cool grass stalks, making a snow angel without any snow.

The anxious looks of his friends were replaced with smiles. Joe stretched out his hand to help Iz to his feet.

'Thanks,' said Iz. 'God, no one else lost their board. You're all flipping brilliant. I do feel like a prat.'

'Oh, of course. You didn't see any of us landing, did you?' said Joe, with a smile playing around the corners of his mouth.

Chris interrupted him.

'Obviously we were brilliant. I landed smooth as a – as a very smooth thing.'

Helen and Joe giggled. Chris, Iz realised on looking more closely, was heavily stained with grass and earth; glancing at the others, he saw the same state of dishevelment. In fact, one of Mia's eyes was starting to puff up.

'Actually, Iz, if it makes you feel better, you did learn to do it properly without the board,' said Johan, the only one of them unmarked and unruffled.

'I don't know about "learnt",' said Iz, upright now, and brushing grass off his legs so that his face was hidden. 'Getting there, maybe. Not going to be quite your standard for a while though.'

'Did you hate it?' Johan asked abruptly.

'Well – I don't know,' said Iz, surprised, looking up. 'It was terrifying. I thought I was going to die. But now you come to mention it – no, I didn't hate it. I would have loved parts of it, come to think, who wouldn't, if only I'd known what I was doing . . .' Iz stopped. Johan was beaming broadly.

'Why? What are you . . . ?'

'Well, when you were talking just now about getting better, practising, I was pleased because – it sounded like it had grabbed you. You weren't just saying, thank God that's over. I love flying, and I thought, all of you being thrown in at the deep end like that, it might put you off for life. And you, Iz, struck me as being quite a natural.'

'Really?' said Iz, 'I thought I was pants. Worse than everyone in the end.'

The others, standing around and listening intently to this conversation, clamoured in denial.

'You looked really good, Iz, honest,' said Helen. 'Dead exciting to watch.'

'Yeah, Iz, she's right,' said Joe, giving him a shove.

'Scary, but almost professional,' put in Chris.

'You were good, I think, but you took many unnecessary risks,' said Mia after careful consideration.

Johan held up his hands, still trying to speak, and everyone quietened down.

'I was going to say, Iz, you only lost the board because, at the end of the day, it's a bit of an encumbrance for a flyer.'

Something else had occurred to Iz. Johan was speaking as if Iz would be able to carry on perfecting his flying. But it only worked 'in this environment', Johan had said. What did that mean? That they would be here much longer than they hoped? That they would never leave? That they could come back another time? He opened his mouth, but Johan shook his head minutely, so that the others didn't even notice, and Iz closed it again.

They were standing in a little circle on the wide flat top of the hill, and now they were really here, not high above it, they found it much larger than they had thought.

A cool night breeze broke around their shoulders, fanned their cheeks, lifted their hair. It seemed to have no connection with the screaming windrush they had felt high up in that dark sky.

Helen glanced around.

'Where are we, Johan? And why? Any ideas?'

'We're on Pilsdon Pen,' said Johan. 'Why, I'm not entirely sure. In what you would call "real" terms, we're not far from the house.'

'It's rather lovely. At least, it would be in the daylight. It's maybe just because it's so much better than feeling like you're stuck underground,' said Helen, with a little shiver of disgust at the memory.

'No, it is really nice, Helen, you're right,' said Iz. 'I know it would have felt good to touch down anywhere after that flight. But when I saw it, waiting, I felt . . .' he looked down, 'I almost *loved* it. For being there. I don't know,' he finished up awkwardly.

'It's got a good feeling,' Joe agreed, looking around, and Chris nodded.

Mia's voice made a formal interjection.

'Excuse me, but isn't this where the skull was found, originally?'

'Yes, you're right, Mia,' said Helen. 'We were talking about it with Miss Ermine, weren't we? She said it was an Iron Age burial mound.'

'Well, it is a theory that the skull came from here to the house a long time ago,' said Johan, 'and it makes sense. Probably someone was wandering about here when the house was being built and found it kicking around and thought, nice souvenir . . .'

Helen snorted, and started to giggle.

'Johan! I wish you wouldn't say "kicking around". I could just see someone booting it along like an old tin can, and no, no one would think, nice souvenir. It's *not*. It's a *skull* . . .'

The others were laughing now, not so much at the image Helen described, but at Helen herself. Her face had gone pink, and her eyes swam and dripped with tears.

Even Johan was laughing, while trying to explain himself. But no one was listening.

Mia was the first to speak, being the only one still in control of her breathing.

'I am not sure that I agree with you, Helen, about it not

being a good souvenir. I think it would be very interesting.'

'True,' said Joe, 'I'd be quite proud of showing it off, if I had one. It's not everyone has a skull in the living room, or wherever.'

'I can see what you mean,' said Iz thoughtfully.

'So can I, but I think my mum would have a fit,' said Chris. 'My dad opened up the fireplace when we first moved to our house, and there was a skeleton of a bird in there, but it was sort of preserved, like a mummy, and I thought it was really neat and wanted to keep it in my bedroom, and for some reason, she just went completely mad.' He shook his head in wonder.

Helen had calmed down now, and looked thoughtful.

'This is a human skull, remember. I don't think that's very nice as a sort of ornament. Imagine if it was your gran, or something. You wouldn't like people to treat her old bones like that, would you? My mum went mad about people just pinching flowers off Grandad's grave. They nick the vases too. It gets you really cross. What if they pinched your relative's skull and popped it on their mantelpiece?'

'Yeah, but this is thousands of years old, right, Johan?' asked Iz.

'Supposed to be,' said Johan.

'I don't know it makes any difference really, does it?' said Helen.

Chris interrupted, 'This is all very interesting, and we could go on about whether mummies should be in museums and so on, but I'd like to know: how important is this skull really, Johan? If it's supposed to be magical, with powers to hold back disaster, and it screams and so on, and you have to get it back, you don't sound – well, exactly *respectful* of it. And it did seem to be the reason we all got stuck here, after all.'

Johan put his head on one side and did the sort of squirming they recognised as a symptom of his difficulty in explaining something. They waited patiently.

'I never said the skull was magical, or screamed or any of that stuff,' said Johan. 'As far as I'm concerned, it's a bit of someone who died a long time ago. But it has to be in place, you know that.'

'What will happen when the skull is back?' asked Joe. 'Is this supposed to change us, or something? Or are we important in – I don't know – *getting* the skull? I'm sure you could have got it without us.'

'I should have been able to get it without you. But the net wanted you here too. Yes, it might be about changing. But I would say, it's more about finding the real people that you are, not changing anything. It is a very unusual occurrence for the net to suck you in like this. The future, an important part of the design, must be in real danger for something like this to happen.'

'Do you mean, like, a catastrophe? Huge bombs, biological attacks, end of world stuff?' asked Chris, fascinated.

Johan smiled.

'The trouble with humans,' he said, 'is they think the whole world is Them. End of humans: end of world. No, Chris, for all we know, it might just be that you, or Helen, or any of you for that matter, has to end up on a platform, on a particular day, precisely two minutes too late to catch the train you had intended, because if you don't, you won't have the right timing and attitude to make people react, or events happen as a result, which means that three months later, a very obscure sort of beetle doesn't become extinct after all. You see,' he said, eyeing Chris's confusion and disappointment, 'it all depends on where you're looking from, as to what you think is important. Depends on your species. But in the end, something like the beetle business could become one little strand in a rope which weaves the net which just misses you and your species out. You never know. If that makes you feel any better. About the importance thing.'

They all stared at him. He was beginning to turn his head this way and that again, sliding from foot to foot.

'But I do sort of know what you mean,' said Helen, after a pause. The others nodded with varying degrees of certainty. You can't see what will come out of it. You just sometimes have to get on with it and trust it'll all work out. Where do you suggest now, Johan? You're getting all twitchy again.'

'Am I? Sorry. Dimension shifters know when an edge is getting close. We certainly need to go down this hill. Let's get going. I'm afraid after that, the net will dictate the exact details of our path.'

They turned and followed him, passing their abandoned boards amidst the grass. Chris waved rather fondly at his.

'Wonder where mine went,' said Iz rather wistfully, gazing up at the small scudding clouds and the moon which shone so brilliantly.

'Probably dropped out of the sky and landed on a rabbit,' said Joe. 'Careless of you, Iz.'

'However, the rabbit was probably a robot one, packed with lethal explosives by some terrorist network, hey, Chris, isn't that right?' said Iz, grinning.

'And that's only the half of it,' agreed Chris, stumbling slightly in the dark. 'Wow, steady now; it's those ridges we saw from above. I didn't realise they were this huge. Like – like moats or something!'

They clambered down an almost perpendicular drop, clutching bracken, until they found themselves at the bottom of what felt like a huge ditch. The other side towered above them. Moonlight just lit the top of it, but here at the base, they were in inky shadow, and felt the ground squelching beneath their feet. A strong, peaty smell rose to their nostrils, and they were uneasily reminded of the giant fungi.

'It's OK,' Johan called back, almost invisible in the gloom ahead, 'just try and climb out of these, and walk along the ridges a little way. We'll get to the bottom in the end.'

It was difficult scrambling up the other side through scrub without being able to see. They were keen to get out, however. Something about the bottom of those great ditches made their hair prickle and their skin crawl. Iz's trainer hit something like a large stone, but it bounced away lightly, invisibly in the dark, leaving him with an uncomfortable feeling that it might have been a skull, and they might, indeed, be wading through a graveyard.

They floundered on, grabbing one another to help, or seeking support. Helen or Joe gave Mia an extra pull now and again. Helen worried about her eye, which must have caught a stone when Mia tumbled from her board on landing, but Mia flapped her away, unconcerned.

'Out of the ridges, now,' Johan called back, 'and on to the lower flank. There is a sort of path. Watch the little streams and marshy bits though, you can't see them.'

Joe and Iz were now right behind him; they could feel that they were heading downhill at last. They took a step, felt their feet land on something like a mattress, felt water rise up around their shoes, then their ankles. Iz gasped, almost speechless with terror. The strange spongy sensation of the ground brought decomposing bodies into his mind; the liquid around his ankles, glittering blackly, was blood. Joe cursed.

'You can see the flipping marsh grass, if you look, Iz. That's where the worst of it is. I keep noticing it *after* I tread in the water.'

Iz let out a breath, swallowed. He loved Joe for his everyday talk. It had saved him from making a screaming fool of himself. He never had liked the dark, but then neither did Joe, and he was coping. He reminded himself that this was a *good* place. He had felt it in his bones, the moment he had laid eyes upon it. Taking a deep smooth lungful of moonlit air, he knew it; his instincts were right this time. His stupid imagination was trying to rattle him. He wouldn't let it happen again.

The others made steadier progress and were some way behind.

'All right?' Joe called back, eyeing Mia's stiff and stumbling gait across the rough ground.

'Fine,' called Chris, 'you keep going. Call back if you see anything.'

Perhaps we won't, thought Joe, perhaps we'll just walk on back to the house. That would be nice.

Johan rounded a slight bend, and, with Joe and Iz almost on his heels, stopped dead in his tracks. He didn't have to explain why. Standing across the path in front of them, the great length of its body and tail blue-silvered with moonlight, turning its huge head towards them, was a black panther.

CHAPTER SIXTEEN

Johan flung back both his arms instinctively to stop the boys, but he need not have bothered. Both Joe and Iz stopped so suddenly, their toes hit the front of their trainers. Without a thought or a word, hearts pressing at their throats with terror, they spun round and raced back the way they had come. Hurtling up the suggestion of a path, they were oblivious to the others picking their way down.

In the confusion, Joe sideswiped Chris, who teetered for a moment on one foot and then crashed to the ground; Joe, thrown off balance by the collision, fell headlong. Iz, with barely a pause in his fluid stride, sidestepped Joe's body and, finding himself face to face with Mia, managed to grab her shoulders; only by pushing her backwards did he prevent a head-on collision. Helen grabbed his arm.

'Stop, would you! What the—?' she began.

There was a pause. Chris and Joe picked themselves up, gasping.

Iz and Joe, remembering the reason for their flight, spun around and looked back down the path. No huge cat was leaping after them. Johan appeared, walking unhurriedly.

'Oh flip,' said Joe, 'what were we thinking of? Even *I* know you're not supposed to run away from big cats.'

'Big cats?' said Chris nervously.

Iz ignored him.

'What do you mean, you're not supposed to run away? What are you supposed to do? Stand there and offer yourself for its tea?' he asked, glaring at Joe.

'Well, it stands to reason, doesn't it?' said Joe, eyeing the approaching figure of Johan. 'You're hardly going to outrun it. Running away just *makes* it chase you. You'd stand more chance just keeping still.'

'Big cats?' asked Helen insistently, her large blue eyes opening a little wider.

'And then what happens?' continued Iz.

Joe waved his hand airily. 'Well, you hope it hasn't noticed you . . .'

'It was flipping staring at us!'

'Or you hope it's already eaten. Or you try shouting at it – like with a dog you think is a bit dodgy.'

Iz was saved from further comment by Johan's arrival.

Helen appealed to him.

'What are they on about, Johan? Is there a big cat down there?'

'Yes, there is, and it's bigger than most I've seen. Inconvenient. All the Professor's fault for messing around with his genetics. It just takes one little slip, and the countryside is full of them.'

Joe was staring at him.

'I thought they were from where people let their pets go, when the law changed, and you had to have a licence.'

'Well, that didn't help matters, no,' said Johan.

'Is it tame?' asked Chris.

'Of course it's not flipping tame,' said Iz, 'it's wandering about here in the night. You heard what Johan said. They escaped, they've bred. These are wild, now.'

'It's just, Johan didn't seem very bothered,' said Chris, defensively.

'Johan's never very bothered,' said Iz in irritation.

'Johan doesn't see death as a particular problem, in case you haven't noticed,' Helen put in quietly.

Johan scratched at one cheek idly and looked at the floor. Helen's final comment seemed to throw everyone into silence. After a moment, Johan looked up at them.

'Yes, it, or rather she, is dangerous. Or potentially. She should have chased Iz and Joe though, and she didn't. When I just stood there, she turned back and mooched away up the path.'

'What do we do now?' Iz asked, calmer, a little embarrassed about his reaction.

'We go on. We'll listen out. She's ahead of us, at least, not behind us.'

For the moment, thought Joe, who knew about animals. Easy enough for her to double back, circle round behind us. Or lie up on the ridge above us. That was their style.

They continued along the tussocky path, strung out in a rather wary line behind Johan. He moved confidently but soundlessly; cautious about catching up with a large predator, they trotted to catch up every so often. The moon kept disappearing behind clouds, which seemed to be getting larger and more numerous, and then they would be plunged into gloom, and Johan would vanish for a moment.

Iz and Joe were the most wary as they turned the corner which had led to their face-to-face encounter with the creature, but they soon saw that the path was empty. Joe scanned anxiously left and right, but could see very little in the darkness. He knew that a big cat could hide itself a few metres from you in cover less dense than this. He felt fairly safe, bunched together with Johan and Iz; it was unlikely that the cat would spring at their little group.

Tagging along at the back, that would be dangerous, he thought. It would be on the lookout for a straggler, a weakling, and a gap between us so we'd be unable to protect it. He stopped, looked back. Behind them came Mia, Chris and Helen in single file, with a fair gap between each. Joe wasn't an organiser. He wasn't sure what to say. Iz, ahead of him, sensed that his friend had stopped and looked back.

'Johan, hold on a minute,' he hissed softly, then called back over his shoulder to Joe: 'What's up, mate?'

'I don't think we should be in a line like this. I don't want to worry the others, but . . .'

Johan interrupted.

'No, you're right. I should pay more attention. We can't walk more than two abreast on this path though. Let's get into twos or threes or something.'

By now the others had closed the gap between them, and were listening for instructions. Johan decided that Iz, Joe and Helen could take the lead, with Chris and Mia following, while he took up the rear. Joe seemed satisfied with this, and he and Iz promised not to bolt if they saw anything.

They continued downhill, more slowly now, as the moon

was snatched from them by increasing cloud. Iz and Helen were just slightly ahead of Joe as they approached part of the path which was hemmed in by large, dark bushes. They jostled together nervously; there wasn't really room for more than one person at a time. Iz stumbled in the dark and found his hair pulled by branches. Just at that moment, all light from the moon disappeared, and they were instantly plunged into the darkest night.

All of them stopped simultaneously. Iz found himself holding one of his hands near to his eyes to find out if he could see it, because he had never known darkness like this. His eyeballs hurt with the strain of trying to see something, anything at all. He could make out the gleam of his palm, if he held it very close to his face.

Chris heard Johan reminding him that if he waited, his eyes would get used to the dark and he would be able to see more. He knew he was right, but he couldn't really believe it. Mia had been somewhere on his left-hand side, on the path, and he put out a hand and found cold skin, an arm. He felt her jump, and the arm was snatched away.

'It's all right, Mia, it's me, Chris. Just checking you're still there.'

'I think I am, though I can't see me,' came back Mia's voice.

'You're there, all right. I felt your arm. Let's keep still till the moon comes out again.'

Further up the path, Iz felt Joe pull his T-shirt. He heard the voices of Johan, Chris and Mia behind them. Why did he feel like he had to be quiet? It would be much more sensible to talk. He licked his dry lips and heard his voice as a strangled squeak.

'Joe? All right?'

'Can't see a thing. Not even where to put my feet.'

'No, well hang on a bit. Helen – are you OK?'

'Yes, I don't mind the dark. But this is different. Out on this hill. With a . . .'

There was an unmistakeable low growl, like thunder. It wasn't like a dog's – it had the rumble of huge machinery, cogs clicking and grinding, in a great, deep cave. It reverberated through their chests, shook their hearts. They had grown up with it on television documentaries, and knew it immediately for what it was. It was the growl of lions on the plains of Africa, of tragic tigers in the dying corners of their kingdom, of the last leopard passing in the night, a silent angel of death, through a slumbering village of huts.

It spoke Death.

It was the most terrifying thing they had ever heard, and they heard it now, in the blackness, far from any escape. The growl came again – surely a little closer, and this time, it took the hairs on the back of their necks and arms and lifted them, and ran a frost through every blood vessel in their bodies.

Iz and Joe wanted to run, but found their feet stuck uselessly to the ground. The sound seemed to have made invisible chains which held them fast, and had melted the bones in their kneecaps.

Helen went first.

She spun, and though Iz could not see her properly, he felt her hair lash across his face. Her movement was enough to free him from the hold of terror. He turned, grabbing Joe's T-shirt and pulling him so that they nearly collided in the dark.

Thank God, thank you thank you, ran through Iz's head as the moonlight magically reappeared, and the whole area was bathed once more in a cold glow which lit Helen's flying hair like a torch as she hurtled off the track and uphill. He sprang after her.

Helen stopped abruptly, screamed, and spun round again, running straight into Iz, smacking him in the nose so painfully with her elbow that he thought it might be broken, and he doubled over, clutching it in his hand.

His cry seemed to bring Helen to her senses, and she stopped, just in time to avoid Joe, who had spread his arms wide as if to stop a horse.

'Whoa, hold up there, Helen. Just steady on a bit,' he said.

'Is it coming? I saw it, right there,' said Helen nervously, sidling towards Joe and looking back the way she'd come.

'The cat?' Iz straightened up, alarmed, still rubbing his nose.

'What? No, a rat, I think. When I ran in the bracken.'

'For God's sake, girl, you'd get us all killed for a rat! The flipping panther is just behind us and we've ended up right back practically in its mouth. I thought the idea was to get away from it.'

'I . . .' Helen didn't know what to say. She had been absolutely terrified, as terrified as anyone, when she heard that growl. She was on the path, out in front, nearer to it than the rest. So she had run. But when she'd seen the rat – running, she would swear to it, *towards* her through the bracken – she hadn't been able to think for a moment. She'd simply turned and run again. And could have run into jaws and claws of something which really could hurt her.

Iz looked back down to the path. There was no cat waiting for them. Chris, Mia and Johan were looking up at them.

'It's OK, Helen,' he said. 'It's not come after us, anyway. Let's just all calm down a minute, and get back down to the path. Come on.'

'Your nose is bleeding,' said Helen slightly huffily as she followed him, Joe politely waiting to assume a protective, rear-guard position.

'I'm sorry,' said Iz, 'I'll tell it not to, in future, when you hit me.'

'What happened there?' Chris called as they reappeared from the bracken.

Iz explained.

'We did hear it,' said Chris sympathetically, 'and it's something else, isn't it, out here in the pitch black? I was so scared. But I couldn't run in any case. My legs wouldn't move.'

'You say you saw a *rat*?' asked Johan.

'Well, it was too big for a mouse. I tell you, I can't help it. I just hate them and . . .' said Helen defensively.

'No, no,' said Johan quickly, 'I'm not having a go at you. I'm just not sure it was a rat. I'm very pleased it was there, though; you might have blundered straight on top of that big cat, on the route you took. Mind you, I have a feeling there will be no avoiding her. It's just, it would be nice to approach her in a balanced way . . .'

'What do you mean, no avoiding her?' asked Chris, sounding suspicious.

'I saw a mouse,' said Mia suddenly, almost conversationally.

No one had thought about how she might react to the threat of a mauling by a wild cat. Now they looked at her, and realised she was as calm as Johan.

'But you say you saw a rat, Helen,' she added, then, insistently, 'I saw a mouse earlier, remember?'

Helen eyed her curiously. Part of her felt that Mia was calm because she didn't understand the danger. Part of her felt that Mia was concentrating too much on irrelevant things like mice. But something pulled at the corner of her memory. It was a little odd, wasn't it?

'I remember. You were right. I saw it too. But I thought then it was bigger.'

'Bigger.' Mia sounded thoughtful. Then she went on, slowly:

'I called it a mouse because I don't know another word for it. I know what a rat is like, and I didn't see that. But I have to say I lied when I said mouse, because it wasn't that either. You say "bigger". What I saw was – longer. Is that the same as your "bigger"?'

'Sort of,' said Helen, 'and you're right, if I think about it. It is longer, really, not just bigger exactly. And I think it *was* the same thing that was in the dice room.'

'I saw something like that as I was coming in to land,' said Iz suddenly. 'I had it as a rabbit, but it wasn't quite right. It's funny how you just decide it has to be something you know, if you can't work out what it really is. What? What are you smiling at, Johan?'

'He knows what it is!' said Joe. 'Don't you?'

'It's not – dangerous, is it?' asked Chris. Johan might be smiling, but he was a bit odd when it came to danger.

'No, no, quite the opposite. I think it's keeping an eye out, trying to help. Do you know what a weasel or a stoat looks like?' he asked Mia and Helen. They shook their heads.

'I do,' said Joe, 'but that's not much use as I didn't notice the thing they keep talking about.'

'Well, what's it like?' asked Iz, turning to Joe impatiently. 'It's one of those whippy little things, isn't it, sharp teeth, eats bunnies?'

Joe looked at the girls and thought for a moment.

'I can't believe you don't know. Well, er, have you seen a ferret? You *must* have,' he added, as Helen looked doubtful, 'Trigger keeps them, he brought them into school that day we were allowed, remember?'

'Yes! Oh, of course, I know. Mia, you remember, don't you? I'm sure everyone saw them. Furry. White but a bit yellow. And one with sort of black and grey.'

'Yeah, that's right,' said Joe, delighted that his attempt to help seemed to be working, 'they call that one a polecat.'

Mia nodded.

'I remember. Smell. But this one we have seen is not as big as that.'

'No, but is it *like* that? Sort of long, say, this big, and brown, perhaps?' Joe held his hands out.

The girls looked closely, looked at each other, and nodded.

'Yes. Could be,' said Helen. 'What is it then? A weasel, you said? What was the other name?'

'A stoat. That seems more the size that you saw. Johan, why do you keep laughing?' Joe's confidence teetered. 'If you know what it is, stop taking the mickey.'

Johan immediately adopted a serious expression.

'I'm not laughing at you, Joe. It's just you are all so near the truth, and I can't believe you don't see it.' He paused. 'I am in a difficult position, you see.'

'Stop beating around the bush if you know something, Johan,' said Iz. 'You're always on about not wasting time gabbing on. And unless you know different, that blur thing is going to pop up again any minute, isn't it, and shove us somewhere – let me guess – straight at puss cat, I'll bet? We don't have all day; or rather, night.'

'The difficult position,' said Johan, apparently deciding to ignore everything Iz had said, 'is one is not supposed to grass on – er, give away details about – er, other dimension shifters.' He rubbed his chin. They could see the hint of a smile.

'*Other* dimension shifters?' said Iz. 'You mean there are *more* of you freaks out here?'

'Freak yourself, flying boy,' Johan answered, but with no animosity. 'And if any of you thought for half a minute, you'd remember I already mentioned another one *you* brought here from school.'

'Miss Ermine!'

Helen hopped about and clapped her hands, smiling with delight. Big cats and rats seemed far from her mind.

Mia looked around them, puzzled.

'Oh, *Ermine*,' said Joe, almost to himself.

Chris was staring at Johan in consternation.

'You mean – she, she can *do* that?' he stammered. 'Turn into another creature?'

Before Johan could answer, Chris raised a shaking finger and pointed at him. 'You, *you* can do that too?'

'It's not a case of "turning into",' said Johan patiently. 'You do a certain amount of dimension shifting to the creature you want – that's putting it very simply – and you just appear to others, in their own dimensions, or realities, to be that creature. That's very different from actually turning into another creature. That, quite obviously, is impossible.'

'Oh, obviously,' said Chris.

'All dimension shifters have favourites. In quite a few, you find it in their taken name. We were a little bit suspicious of Miss Ermine from the start.'

Before anyone else could comment on this, Johan held up his hand. He looked at Iz, and his strange, caramel eyes glittered mischievously.

'And now, what Iz suggested would happen, is happening.' He opened his eyes wide, showing the whites. 'What are you, boy, some kind of mystic?'

Iz looked beyond Johan and felt a sinking sensation as he saw the moonlit landscape blur and disappear. He gazed at Johan levelly.

'No, Johan, I just kind of worked it out, based on previous experience. And don't tell us, let's guess what's behind us.'

Slowly, they all turned round. They saw immediately that they were in fact surrounded, in a perfect circle, walled with shaking nothingness. Crouched uneasily before them was the huge black cat on one side of the path; on the other, mewling and pawing each other, were three duskily spotted cubs.

They all stiffened. Iz felt the moisture drain from his mouth. Somehow, he found his voice, and whispered fiercely, not taking his eyes from the cat for a moment:

'There's a time to joke about, Johan, and – well, this isn't it. I notice you're at the back.'

'I'm entirely confident in you young people and your abilities. You've done all right so far,' Johan's voice hissed back.

The cat kept them fixed with her glowing yellow eyes. They saw her whiskers twitch, each strand lit white by moonlight, and realised that she was curling her lip in the darkness.

Chris, as transfixed as all of them, leant his head slowly back in Johan's direction.

'Can't you change into – I mean, do that thing like Miss Ermine does?' he whispered.

'What? You want me to change into a stoat? So it can play with me like a mouse while you all get away?'

'No, I mean something that would drive it away . . .'

'And what would that be? An elephant, perhaps – I'm not sure I could manage that. Bit out of practice.'

'Johan, you're so—' Iz started to complain, feeling rather sorry for Chris.

'Shhh,' said Johan softly, 'a little patience.'

The cat turned her head away and eyed the cubs, who seemed oblivious to both the blurred edges of their world and the group of people watching them. They saw the planes of her beautiful but terrible face as it turned. The nose was broad, the texture of it, suede. Beneath the great muzzle, her chin jutted like a boxer's fist; she let it drop, panting slightly, and a flicker of light played on the hanging lip. There was a glisten of saliva, a glimpse of a huge white fang in the massive jaw.

Helen felt the terror rooting her to the spot, but another part of her revelled in the creature's beauty. Joe, too, almost forgot his fear for a moment in the awe of standing so close to one of his favourite animals.

The cat turned her gaze back upon them, stiffened suddenly, and crouched. The tip of its incredibly long tail twitched furiously from side to side. They saw the muscles in its shoulders shift slightly in the bluish shadow.

Helen realised that one of them must have startled it. Next to her, to her horror, there was only a space where Mia had been. She looked around, down:

'Mia!'

Her cry was stifled by a hand which pressed across her mouth from behind.

'Quiet. All of you. Say nothing. Don't move.' It was Johan's voice, in a whisper no louder than the sighing of the wind, but they all heard him.

One by one, they became aware of a figure crawling away on all fours in front of them, straight towards the path.

No one dared move. They held in their breath, too terrified for the girl on the ground to make a sound.

Joe watched, torn between fear for Mia and admiration. He thought he knew what she was doing. It might just work. Never between mother and young, though, he thought, willing Mia off the path, willing her to hear his thoughts, never get between mother and young.

Mia was moving in a strange way, not as they would have done if they had been on all fours, thought Iz, biting his lip as he watched. She kept her knees off the ground, for a start, which they would have found awkward. She made it look easy, natural. And she had a sort of swing going, almost a swagger.

Mia was now ambling, in an apparently haphazard way, off the path and directly towards the cubs. The cat had turned its attention away from the group and was staring fixedly at Mia. Still, it made no move.

Joe noticed that Mia was now close to the blurred edge of the circle. She was approaching the cubs from such an angle that they were almost between her and the mother cat. Good girl, he thought, knowing now that her strange route was anything but random.

The cubs, which had seemed so small in comparison to the mother, now looked much larger to Helen as she watched them pause and look up from their play to stare at Mia. Like very big, boisterous puppies, but with more serious claws and teeth.

Chris realised he was as tense as the big cat. He too, was poised to leap. He felt almost sure that it was just a matter of time before the cat was on top of Mia, biting, mauling. He wasn't sure what they could do about it, but he knew he'd have to try something. If Mia was trying to be a distraction, it had worked. The cat was no longer looking at them. Maybe they could distract it from her, in turn.

The cubs had paused, unsure, but Mia started to stride towards them even more confidently in her strangely fluid, four-legged way. Suddenly, one of the cubs trotted out towards her, its tail aloft, ears pricked. Mia met it head down, hair hanging, without pausing for a moment, so that Helen wondered if she had seen it. The cub sidestepped, almost pushed out of the way, and put its cheek down so that Mia's head rubbed it hard in passing. Mia continued as if she had not noticed, and the cub arched its back and cavorted alongside her, aiming a paw at her head.

Iz tore his eyes away from Mia and the cubs and back to the mother cat. Mia seemed to have the cubs, all right. But how would mum cope with this stranger playing with the kids?

The mother cat, still staring at Mia, pulled herself out of her crouch, and sat upright, stretching the long column of her neck as if trying to get a better view. Mia was now butting her way through the cubs, who made way for her, then sported and gambolled about.

Iz turned his head slightly towards Johan.

'What do we do, Johan? I daren't try the screen – I think we'd get the cat's attention again.'

'You might have a job keeping one eye on that and one on the cat,' agreed Johan, 'and you don't need it, anyway. Mia's cracked it, hasn't she?'

'But we've all got to get through. What do *we* do? Mia's nearly there. Mum's OK, at the moment, but she won't be if we all just run through. She'd get one of us, at least.'

He heard Johan sigh.

'I don't understand. Mia's shown you how to do it. What's the problem?'

Helen turned around and looked at him properly, forgetting her plan not to move.

'What, we've got – to do that?'

'Unless you've got a better plan,' said Joe, unexpectedly. 'She's a flipping genius,' he continued, looking at Mia as she boxed a cub away with one arm and stuck stolidly to her route to the far side of the circle. He sank down on to all fours, slowly, and looked up at Helen.

'But it isn't easy. You have to do just like her. Watch her closely. Try and move natural. And very, very brave. Act like you own the place. Don't look at them straight. And not ever at Mum. Just act like she's not there. OK?'

Then he looked away again, and, with little grunts of effort, set off in the same direction as Mia.

Iz, looking down at him, suddenly realised he didn't want to be doing that on his own. He hissed at Johan:

'Will she mind less or more if we go as a bunch?'

'Go all together, but split into one at a time as you go through the cubs,' Johan said softly. 'You don't want her to think they're being mobbed by a gang.'

Obediently, they all crouched and started to follow Joe. Their hearts thumped, but they realised they could feel no more terrified than they were already. In fact, it was slightly better to be moving, taking some action. Joe paused, waited for Iz to draw alongside.

'Try to keep your eye on the cubs without looking right at them. They'll know, and Mum will see, if you look straight at them. Try it – sort of out of the corner of your sight.'

'OK,' Iz whispered back meekly.

'Then, wherever they are, you have to move so you're always this side of them. They are between you and Mum.' The others were behind them now, listening.

'If one of us gets it wrong, with one cub, for a moment, she'll be on us.'

'Right,' muttered Chris.

They set off again. They just caught a glimpse of Mia, waiting at the far edge of the blur wall, on the path; the cubs were playing around her. Then they put their heads down and tried to adopt the resolute movement they had seen. As they approached the halfway point, the cubs broke from their game and loped towards them, curiously.

Somehow, without speaking, they remembered Johan's advice, and by slowing down or speeding up, sorted themselves into a rough line.

Helen tried to keep her eyes on the shadowed, damp grass beneath her hands; her hair was a useful screen so that she could gauge where the cubs were. At least Mum was staying still. She was still craning her neck, but didn't seem too concerned.

She felt a hard thud, and her hair was pressed tightly to her cheek. A little growling cry told her that a cub had just rubbed her face. She pressed onwards, and felt a thwack on her leg from a paw, but there was no painful digging of claws.

Iz felt a claw catch in his hair, and nearly yelped as the cub yanked it free. He felt another swat and saw a greyish underbelly from beneath his fringe. The pain fired him up. He would have loved to play with these things. Instead, he ventured a careful shove with his forearm; he'd seen Mia do that, they seemed to like it, and it stopped them getting too uppity.

Chris took a shaky path behind them. He didn't get how this worked, but he did his best to stick rigidly to the rules, knowing he had no natural aptitude for this game. Barging two cubs rather brusquely out of the way, so that they squealed and the big cat pricked her ears anxiously for a moment, he followed the others past the halfway mark and towards Mia on the far side of the circle.

They curved their awkward way, thigh muscles and hips

aching unbearably, jeans stretching uncomfortably tight, back towards the path. It was like an elaborate game of chess, or etiquette rules of some old-fashioned dance. A cub strolled casually one way; Chris had to stop abruptly, while Helen had to speed up and change direction. Meanwhile another ran to the side of them, then crossed their path and tried to pass between them and the dimension edge. They would try to stop, manoeuvre, change course, sometimes nearly banging shoulders on the blur wall, in order to keep to the rule of all cubs between them and the mother cat at all times. They couldn't help thinking it would be a lot easier if the cubs knew the rule too.

When they reached Mia, squatting casually waiting for them, they looked up and gratefully adopted her crouched, more upright pose. They struggled to get their breath back as the cubs left them alone for a moment, intent in their own fight over a leaf.

'Where's Johan?' whispered Iz suddenly, looking around.

The others did the same.

'I thought he was right behind us,' said Chris, puzzled. 'I don't think he can just get round another way. We all have to get through, don't we?'

Joe was looking at the cubs.

'Weren't there only three of those guys?'

They followed his gaze. Four cubs now cavorted in front of them. One of them seemed to brush the others away. As it came towards them in the half light, it seemed a little bigger; much bigger, in fact. Then they saw floppy hair; the moonlight ran in folds over a T-shirt, sinewy arms stamping down like forelegs on the grass, in a definite, cat way.

'Johan!' they whispered almost simultaneously.

'It's you,' said Iz, patting him on the back. 'Thank God. We had you mixed up with one of the cubs then. Or we were looking at them and you just sneaked up . . .' His voice tailed off. He frowned. 'How did you do that? That was you, wasn't it? You did that thing, didn't you, like Miss Ermine?'

'Did I?' said Johan, grinning at him and sitting up on his haunches. 'Must have been good then. Maybe even Mum saw me like that.'

'Look,' said Helen. The ground between them and the cats was starting to fade. They thought for a moment that the moon was being hidden by cloud again, but then they realised that the bushes, the bracken, the air above, had started to shake and dissolve. The blurred wall had come between them and the animals.

Johan turned to look over his shoulder.

'And look here. It's gone. Our path is clear again.' He stood up slowly and looked down at them. 'What, do you like staying like that?'

Slowly, unused to the feeling that the cat's eyes were no longer on them, they straightened up, rubbing the tops of their legs and flexing their ankles.

'Well done, Mia,' said Joe. 'We wouldn't have thought of that without you to show us.'

Mia looked at him uncertainly, then held out her hand. Joe looked down at it, confused for a moment, then held out his own. She shook hands with him firmly.

'Thank you,' she said.

'No, thank *you*,' said Joe.

'I said that. The same,' said Mia stubbornly.

The others looked at each other; Helen giggled.

'Come on, you two. Let's get on down the path. Is that right, Johan?'

'You've got it. Nearly there now, I think. We haven't taken any detours. Hardest but most direct route. I would expect nothing less, now I know you all better.'

And he turned and led the way, swinging down the path in an almost carefree manner. They followed, a warm glow pushing aside the chill of the night air as they realised the compliment.

CHAPTER SEVENTEEN

Though they were in lighter spirits, partly because Johan's mood was infectious and partly through the exhilaration of escaping the cat and leaving the claustrophobic blur wall behind them again, the group started to feel exhaustion creeping over them for the first time.

Mia periodically touched at the puffy skin around her eye and sucked her breath in with a little hiss. Iz found the weight of his arm seemed to pull on his aching shoulder, which had taken the brunt of his fall from the sky. If the arm swung a little, it hurt even more. He tried folding it across his chest and cupping the elbow with his other hand to keep it still. That worked for a while, but then the shoulder started to complain even more. Helen noticed, and said that it needed a sling, but none of them had a T-shirt to spare. It was cold.

Johan pulled Iz's T-shirt from over his stomach, folded it up and over so his arm was trapped against his chest, and tucked the end of it into the neckline. It didn't feel very secure to Iz, but there wasn't enough material to knot it. The pain settled down again, but now his back and stomach were freezing, and, unaccountably, the bruise on his jaw from Chris's fist started to throb. He had forgotten all about their fight. It seemed so long ago.

Helen ached all over; her legs, especially, dragged along like wood, reminding her that they were unaccustomed to climbing, to holding her steady on a board in high wind, to propping her on all fours.

Chris was in much the same condition. The lip, which Iz had split with a punch, had swollen and felt huge. He licked it experimentally from time to time and tasted the metal of dried blood in his mouth.

It seemed a long walk. Iz glanced up at the night sky. There didn't seem to be any change. Did dawn ever come, here?

They felt the ground level out, and as they rounded the base of the deep slope, they saw the lake spread out below them, sparkling and tranquil in the moonlight. They stopped and let out a cry of recognition.

'But if that's the lake,' said Helen, puzzled, 'the house should be just . . . Oh.'

They followed her pointing finger.

They had never seen the edge of the dimension so far away, but they recognised it immediately. Where the house should have been, there was simply a shaking haze, stretching as far as the eye could see, up into the dark night sky, apparently without end.

Johan wasn't really looking. He was standing with his back to them, a little way ahead, hands on hips, gazing at the lake.

'Well, we can't just amble back in to bed then,' said Chris, disappointed. 'Though I suppose I never thought we could.'

'The skull,' Helen reminded him. 'I think we have to find the skull first.'

They looked at the motionless figure of Johan, his outline frosted in moonlight. He suddenly looked very boyish again.

Iz moved up behind him.

'Johan.'

The figure turned, the face shadowed.

'The skull's in the lake, isn't it?'

Johan nodded.

'What's the plan?'

'I suppose I try and get it again. Maybe with all of you here now, I'll be able to. Don't forget, I don't know much more than you.'

'Well, do we just stand here? Should we wade in and feel around or something?' asked Helen, eyeing the waters.

'If it's on the bottom. I mean, it could be anywhere in there,' put in Chris. 'Won't it take forever? How deep is it? I know you're – different, Johan, but can you see all right? Breathe, without gear?'

'Even I have limitations,' sighed Johan. 'I feel I should know exactly where it is. I'm waiting for inspiration.' He gazed back across the surface of the water, where a light breeze was rippling the surface.

Helen shivered. It looked very cold. Reeds and vegetation blurred where bank ended and water began.

Mia had been listening carefully. Now she stood a few metres from Johan and imitated his gaze.

'Three?' she said doubtfully, turning slightly to Johan, and then to Joe.

'Three?' echoed Johan, eyeing her with his head on one side like a bird.

Joe saw Mia's confusion, the appeal in her eyes. He knew she might give up on her idea if someone didn't understand quickly.

'Three, Mia? Can you explain a bit more?' She'd said that number before, again and again. Why was it important to her? When had she said it? Maybe it was just something she liked to say. But she certainly hadn't said it all the time. Not since . . .

'Pretty. You said flag. It's not a flag. A flower. Three big petals. Three more inside. Three on a branch. Everything, three.'

'Oh!' said Joe, thumping his thigh, making Mia jump back, startled. 'Sorry, Mia. I just remembered. In the Professor's study. We were looking at the flags. Yellow ones. My mum likes – liked them.'

'Flags?' Johan queried. Then his brow cleared. 'Irises! Of course. I haven't heard them called flags for years. There were some in the study, were there? Yes, I suppose there were. I remember. They grow here in the lake—'

Mia made a little sound of exasperation, pulled Johan's arm and pointed.

'I see them. There's just one clump in flower,' said Joe.

'All very well, but does that help?' asked Chris, in an irritable voice.

Iz was pulling at his lower lip.

'Bit of a coincidence. She's not suggesting the Professor lobbed the skull in there and stopped to pick a few flowers for his study while he was at it, is she?'

'The Professor certainly didn't lob it anywhere. He wasn't even here. We don't know who chucked it, but I've told you, I don't think that's very important at the moment. But the irises – everything for a reason,' said Johan firmly, 'and I don't understand why, and I don't care, but *that* feels right. The skull is probably caught up in that clump.'

'Well,' said Helen, 'we've got to start somewhere, and that's as good a place as any. It gives us something to go on.'

'Us?' said Johan. 'It's me that's got to pick it up, I should think. Nothing for you to worry about. Let's get round to that edge and I'll wade in.'

'Oh,' said Helen, 'OK.' She felt relieved that she wouldn't have to get in there after all, but strangely uneasy. After all they had been through, surely it couldn't be as simple as this?

They picked their way down to where they could see the pale blobs of flower petals, colourless in the moonlight, seemingly floating in the air above massy, long green tongues of leaves, which flourished out of the water near the bank.

Johan pulled off his ancient trainers and gingerly felt his way into the water. His foot made a dull splash as he entered, and the ripples hurried away across the surface of the lake. Another step and he was in, the water just above his waist.

'Brrr! Right,' he said, 'I'll feel around as best I can from here, and then if I don't get it, I'll dive under and see what's there.'

He had just started to part the stems, when Helen heard Iz, next to her, let out a single, very crude oath. Without another sound, he barged her out of the way, nearly knocking her to the ground, and leant over the water, grabbing great, wet handfuls of Johan's T-shirt.

'Get him out!' he screamed, turning to Chris and Joe behind and on either side of him on the bank, 'Get him out NOW!' And as they shook themselves from their shocked immobility and started forward, 'Give us a hand! Don't just stand there!'

Mia shot forward and grabbed Johan's arm; Chris and Joe, slipping and half-wading, pulled at the parts of his T-shirt closest to them. 'Keep out of the water! Both of you, for Christ's sake!' shouted Iz. Helen forgot her indignation and hung on to the back of the waistband of Iz's jeans, keeping him on the bank. Johan, startled, put his own effort into regaining the bank, and struggled out.

'What—?'

'Up the bank, up further,' insisted Iz, staring at the water, dragging and pushing at the others as they stood gasping and dripping, 'A *crocodile*. Huge. I saw it, I tell you. It was coming.'

Helen put her hands over her face. Chris and Joe put theirs on top of their heads. They reeled with the shock.

I knew it, thought Helen, I knew all along. She looked up again from her hands, and stared at the water closest to them. The others suddenly had the same thought and did the same, backing a little further up the bank. Johan's shoulders sagged and he looked at the ground, still slightly out of breath, wiping water droplets from his nose.

'Where did you see it, exactly?' he asked Iz.

Iz pointed.

'Just there. The back, the tops of the eyes, the nose. If it hadn't been for those, I would have thought it was a log or something.' He glanced behind them, towards the distant blur.

'We're not being surrounded yet. It's not forcing us in.'

'No, and maybe it won't, this time. I still think this is my problem.'

'We must be here to help, surely, Johan,' said Helen. She hoped Chris wasn't going to suggest Johan took on the appearance of some other creature to get through this. Nothing much would get past a crocodile, would it?

'What if there's more?' said Joe suddenly.

'I suppose there might be,' said Johan.

'It would help if we knew,' said Chris. 'Can we try the screen here?'

'No reason why not,' agreed Johan, but he didn't sound very hopeful. He stared out across the water, keeping watch, as everyone huddled further up the bank, all except Mia, as usual, closing their eyes.

'It's here,' she announced calmly. 'There is the lake, just like it is here.'

They opened their eyes and saw her gazing avidly at the translucent oblong floating just in front of her.

'How many, first, that's what I'm worried about,' said Chris firmly.

The real-time image of the lake faded and was replaced by an oval outlined in blue. A short brown line appeared with a slight 'ping' in the centre of the oval. Nothing else happened.

'I take it that's our croc,' said Chris, 'and there seems to be only one. He's shown dead centre here. He could be, I suppose, but I think this is just to show numbers of creatures, not necessarily where he is . . .'

'Where he is would be pretty darned useful,' said Joe.

A red circle appeared around the brown line; there was a pause, then both disappeared for a second, reappearing near one of the blue edges of the lake diagram.

'Well done, Joe. I reckon that's him,' said Helen. 'And I think that edge is where we are, don't you?'

There was a pause as they tried to think what to ask next. Helen turned to Joe.

'You know about animals, Joe. Anything about these? Anything scare them off?'

Joe shook his head.

'I don't know much. Just what you see on telly. Only the same as you'd know.'

'But I don't watch those programmes usually,' said Helen, 'I don't watch telly much at all. There's either too much to do in the house, or I'm out. I wouldn't remember much they said in any case.'

Chris looked at Joe.

'Aren't they reptiles, Joe?'

'Yes,' Joe nodded, staring thoughtfully at the screen.

'That makes them rely on the sun's heat, doesn't it, to move and so on. Don't they slow down if they get cold?'

'Good point. It's not that warm in the water, is it? I'm not sure if it's cold enough though. To actually stop it. And Iz saw it moving.'

'I did,' said Iz, who hadn't said much because he was finding it hard to concentrate. He knew Johan was keeping a lookout, but he felt he still had to keep checking the water.

He imagined Johan being suddenly snatched, silently, from right next to them.

'Anything else?' Chris asked in desperation.

'They won't attack anything if they've eaten already,' said Joe suddenly, 'I do remember that.'

'I wonder if we can check if it's hungry,' said Iz.

The screen gave its little 'ping' sound again, and showed some kind of gauge in the bottom corner. A red level showed up to half way.

'Well,' said Helen, 'I'm not quite sure what that's supposed to be, but I guess it could be its energy levels, or how full up it is, or something, couldn't it?'

'Yes,' said Iz, 'and it doesn't look very helpful. I don't think it's cold enough and I don't think it's well fed enough to rule out an attack. If we had a way of making the lake colder, or of giving it a sheep or something, we might be on to something.'

They waited. No change happened on the screen in front of them.

'No artificial systems here, then, to fix the temperature, or dose it with food,' sighed Chris.

To their surprise, the tray slowly turned over, shook, shimmered, and disappeared.

'Well!' said Helen. 'Looks like there's a time limit on the thing. What are we supposed to do now?'

'No time limit,' Johan called up to them. 'You bring it up, you keep it there – but it's a strain, though you might not notice. You've run out of things to ask it.'

'Is there – is there a way of moving which might be safe?' Helen asked tentatively, looking around the faces of the others. 'I mean, like Mia did with the cats.'

'I thought they had tiny brains,' Chris offered. 'A killing machine, like a shark.'

'No, no,' said Joe, an offended note in his voice, 'they're not like that. Nor are sharks for that matter. Crocodiles – they look after their babies just as well as that mother cat. There's more to them than you think. There was a programme I watched not long ago, where a bloke swam down and sort of pinched under this crocodile's chin, and lifted it up, and it was sweet as pie with him.'

Iz looked at him blankly.

'I don't fancy it, personally. Anything – well, a bit less hands-on, that you remember?'

'See what you mean,' Joe admitted. 'Um – well there was another programme, and the bloke there waded up to loads of them, and he just splashed at them when they got a bit close. That's what they do to each other.'

Chris looked doubtful.

'I would have thought splashing brought them to you. I mean, if some animal went in there, surely the croc would come to eat it because it splashed about? And I thought they attacked and killed each other every so often anyway.'

'Most animals wouldn't splash about when they came to drink, would they?' Joe pointed out. 'The thing is, not to act like its prey. To act like another crocodile. And they only attack smaller crocodiles.'

'How big was it, Iz?' asked Chris.

'I only saw the length. And the width, I suppose. Longer than any of us, than Johan. It seemed big enough at the time, I can tell you.'

Johan called up, hearing his name.

'All right, you lot? Any plan? Otherwise, I think I'll just risk it. You keep an eye out, and I'll jump out sharpish if you see something.'

'It'll move a lot quicker than you, Johan,' Joe called back to him, and then hurried down the bank. 'Is there no other way you can think of? Do you have to get it right now?'

'I do, really,' said Johan, quietly.

The others came up behind Joe, keeping their eyes on the glittering surface of the lake. Every time a breeze fanned the ripples, they thought they could see a long back, perhaps a tail.

'Right,' said Iz, 'then I think we'll go with what we know from Joe. And a bit from Chris. If two of us spread out away from Johan, and stir the water a bit at the edge, gently, with – um – long sticks if we can find them, that might make it come and have a look, thinking it's something better to eat than a stringy bloke.'

Johan flashed him a charming smile.

'Then two of us stay near to Johan. They keep lookout, and if it rushes in for the kill, both of them try Joe's splash thing. If the two are together, he might think it's a pretty big crocodile.'

'Hmm,' said Johan, 'I like it. It's a kind of plan A and plan B, all in one. Who's doing which particular bit?'

They looked at each other. Helen didn't much like the sound of any of it, but she decided quickly that she preferred the long stick approach.

'I'll pretend to be a – a sheep or whatever it eats, if that's all right with everyone else. I'll get sticks.' She headed for the only bush or tree she could see, an elder, and started breaking branches from it and stripping leaves.

With very little discussion, Chris and Mia soon had a long, bendy stick each; Iz seemed to have appointed himself protector-in-chief of Johan; Joe, feeling he had to back his own idea, and sure he could make a convincing splash, decided to be the other half of a large crocodile, if necessary.

Mia, Helen and Chris took up strategic positions further along the bank, on either side of where Johan would be searching. Once they had started stirring the water gently, Iz and Joe squatted on the bank above the clump of irises, finding that they could judge the surface of the water better like that.

Johan waded in again, not showing any sign of nerves, and began to push his hands between the leaves and stems of the plant, feeling underwater as far as he could. Iz watched his shoulder disappearing, his face turned sideways just above the surface, imagining the sudden jerk from the murky depths, Johan vanishing, perhaps without even time to scream. What good would their plan be then?

Johan waded out deeper, circled the clump. The watchers and the stirrers stared. No one saw any further sign of the crocodile. Yet none of them doubted what Iz had seen. It had shown on the screen.

But, Chris thought, daring to move a little closer to the edge of the bank, what had it shown? Perhaps it was something else. It had been represented by a mere brown line. Perhaps Iz had just seen a very large fish – a pike? Still unpleasant, but not life-threatening. He poked the stick in closer to the bank, testing the depth. It wasn't deep here. The water was so cloudy though, especially from his stirring, that you couldn't see the bottom.

Quite suddenly, without warning, the brown water seemed to rise up in a great wave in front of him. He staggered backwards, seeing a flash of greenish white; he heard a tremendous snap, and found himself staring into a huge, gaping pink mouth, water running from the rows of fangs. He just had time to make sense of what had happened – the white he had seen had been the beast's underbelly as it launched out of the water. It must have been hidden, impossibly, in the shallows right next to him. Then the crocodile moved one leg forward, and Chris, backing up faster than he would have thought possible, smacked at its jaws with the stick.

The crocodile lunged again, upwards. Again there was the terrible, dull snap like a great metal cable breaking, and Chris felt a shock run up his arms. The creature crashed back to earth, a piece of the elder branch clamped in its jaws, and suddenly turned and vanished into the water.

Chris stood, gasping. The wake from the crocodile's dive lapped at the bank, then disappeared as ripples. He looked across at the others. They each stood, still as statues, staring at him. He hardly dared move. Would it try again?

Johan called across the water to him.

'All right, Chris?'

He found his voice.

'I think so. Yes, yes, I'm all right.'

'You want to sit out for a while?'

Chris thought for a moment. Yes he did. But he couldn't.

'No, I'll be all right. At least it's working.'

Mia and Helen both inched a little further back from the bank. Helen dabbled her stick in more gently.

Johan looked up at Iz and Joe.

'I've reached as far as I can. I have to go under now. I'll be as quick as I can.'

Iz nodded. He didn't know how Johan could, not after that. He'd done some pretty stupid things in his time, but he couldn't see himself doing what Johan was doing. He looked across at Joe, who was covering his face in his hands, and gave him a shove with his foot.

'Keep your eyes peeled. Won't see anything like that, will you?' he hissed.

Johan was already underwater when they looked back. They saw his foot break the surface with a splash and winced, imagining the crocodile homing in on the disturbance. He seemed to be down for a long time. Joe shifted uncomfortably. Iz scratched his knee. Too long. They were starting to stand up, determined to do something, when they saw Johan surface with a great splash, his hand above his head, clasping the underside of something round, smooth as a sea-washed rock, dark and shining.

'Got it!'

His hair poured in a soaking cascade around his face. He wiped his eyes and nose with his free hand and blew like a whale.

'Oh brilliant!' said Joe.

'Great! But shhh! You're making such a racket, Johan,' said Iz, scrambling down to help him out. 'Just get out of there quick.'

Johan smiled at him, emerging from the water. Iz watched impatiently. Waist deep, knee deep, ankle deep: still not safe. Finally, both feet were on the edge of the shallow slope of the bank. Iz grabbed his hand.

'Come on, get up here, would you,' he muttered.

Johan smiled again. The skull hung from his hand, glittering, dripping big silver droplets into the water.

'I—'

But that was all he had time to say.

Iz just caught a glimpse of huge open jaws, down near their feet, water gushing inside the pinkish maw as it rushed towards them. There was a reek of rotting fish, then a sound like a car boot being slammed, and Johan was thrown forwards, face down. The skull flew from his hand and landed on the bank near Joe, and in a moment, Johan was being yanked backwards into the water.

'No!' Iz screamed.

Johan's head and shoulders started to disappear, and the water boiled in a frenzy around him. Without a thought, Iz dived after him. He gulped foul-tasting water and choked. Somehow, he found denim, a belt loop slipped around his thumb. He searched frantically beneath the water with the other hand, found another belt loop, and grabbed on tight.

Joe, watching in horror, knew what the boiling water meant. The crocodile was death-rolling, trying to tear a chunk off Johan, or drag him under and drown him.

He had no idea what terrible damage had been done, but he could see that Johan was face down underwater in the shallows, with Iz on top of him. He floundered down into the water, felt for Johan's hair, and pulled his face clear. The eyes were closed, but then they opened, expressionless, and it seemed to Joe that Johan took a breath.

He heard the others scrambling, running along the bank,

heard someone's gasping sobs as they ran, unintelligible words.

Iz gripped on tight to Johan's jeans and pulled himself off his back. He could feel that Johan was still trapped, and was sure the crocodile had the lower part of one of his legs, or his foot. Nothing was moving for the moment. The boiling water had subsided.

'Pull, Iz,' Joe screamed, grabbing Johan underneath the arms and heaving desperately.

'Hold on a minute,' Iz called back, but he was still choking from the mouthful of water he'd taken in, and he wasn't sure if Joe could hear him. 'It's still got him! We'll never get him out by pulling.'

Not all of him, at any rate, he thought. If those jaws let go of whatever they've got, they'll not make a mistake a second time. It'll take both his legs, and probably the rest of him, with one more snap.

Joe paused. Helen was first to reach his side. She was crying.

'Why are you stopping? Get him out! Pull!'

'Shut up, Helen,' said Joe, suddenly angry. Chris and Mia were there too now. Everyone stood very still.

Iz half-crawled along, feeling the length of Johan's legs beneath the water. Suddenly, his hand touched something like a barnacle-covered rock. He snatched his hand back, then cautiously found the rock again, gripped it tight. It was the crocodile's nose.

What the hell was he going to do now, he thought. He couldn't exactly prise its mouth open. He didn't know what else to try. He called back to Joe:

'When I say go, pull as hard as you can. Right up the bank. Don't stop.'

Helen saw Johan blink, dazed.

Iz was about to thump the crocodile's nose when he remembered his own position. If that mouth opened, it was just as likely to close on his head or arm as anywhere else. Then they wouldn't be much better off. He needed to be behind those jaws. He felt along the invisible, gnarled surface of the nose, and half-crawling, half-floating, turned and lined himself up in the water above the creature, keeping a handhold on it. There was its eye, surely. He couldn't believe it didn't move.

Joe couldn't believe it either. He knew that at any moment, it would roll again. Iz now seemed to be on top of it. He would be completely swept under when it went.

'Iz, whatever you're doing, make it quick. If it rolls again, it'll drown you,' he called.

Iz grabbed a mouthful of air, then ducked his head underwater. He wanted the front leg, and he knew that should be right about here, a little too deep for him to keep his face above water.

He kept his eyes open, but only saw brown murk. He found the position of each front leg though, with his hands, and pulled his knees into place behind each one. Then he was sitting upright, clear of the water from the waist upwards, gasping for air on the broad back, feeling the armour plating of the creature sticking through his jeans, amazingly sharp. Now he needed to make it let go. He reached forward, trying to thump its nose, but he couldn't seem to get any force behind it. The water dragged at his movements, slowing them down. He was sure the crocodile had not even felt his attempt.

Joe realised what he was trying to do.

'Wait!' he called to Iz, then turned to Helen. 'Your stick. Give it here.'

But Joe could not let go of Johan's shoulders to take it from her.

'One of you,' Joe improvised. 'For Christ's sake be quick. Hit it on the nose with the stick. If it opens its mouth, everyone pull and keep out of the way.'

Iz heard him and waited. It seemed an age since the creature had attacked. But Chris had grabbed Helen's stick and was rushing towards him.

Chris couldn't see any sign of the crocodile, but he realised Iz must be astride it. He waded in close, and held out the end of the stick towards Iz.

'I can't see its nose!' he shouted, 'can you? Or do you want me to—'

'No, give it here. I know where it is. Get back up ready to pull,' Iz called back, snatching at the end of the stick. He had it! He felt the crocodile shift, ever so slightly, for the first time, and knew he was out of time. With both hands on the stick, he brought it straight down like a pile driver, where he guessed the tip of the creature's nose was.

He saw what looked like a huge, brown, dripping rock rear up from the water in front of his face. It was the top jaw – the mouth had opened.

'PULL!' he screamed, and heard it echoed by voices on the bank.

He turned the branch sideways and leant forward over

the nose, gripping tightly with his calves on the creature's sides, trying to keep his balance. The branch just flicked inside the crocodile's mouth; then, with a tremendous slam, the jaws smashed shut.

Iz had seen people on television who would then pull the closed jaws up towards them, keeping the mouth shut. That part wasn't supposed to be too difficult. But before he could try it, he felt the body beneath him whip sideways, throwing him off, as the creature headed back to deep water. He rolled on his back and ended up almost on the bank. As his feet hit ground, he ended up automatically standing, spluttering water and unable to see, but feeling hands grabbing him, pulling him onwards and upwards. When he could see again, albeit blearily, he made out the shape of Johan, lying on the ground at the top of the bank.

He heard Helen's voice through the bubbling in his ears. 'Are you all right?'

'Is Johan all right?' he asked, spitting out filthy-tasting water.

'He's all right,' said Joe, but Iz didn't believe him.

'His leg. Is his leg all there?'

'He's OK,' said Chris. 'It got the bottom of his jeans. His foot seems to be a bit of a mess, but not from teeth. Joe says it twisted the trouser leg when it rolled and it sort of garrotted his foot. I think it'll be OK. He just took in a bit of water. He's coming round. Sit down.'

Iz was pushed down by urgent hands, next to Johan. Damn that water, he thought, trying to see clearly. Blinking and screwing up his eyes, he eventually saw that Johan was indeed sitting up, and was actually smiling, in between grimacing with pain, even if his lips looked rather blue.

Iz inched across closer to inspect Johan's foot.

At the ankle, there was a deep, red-purple groove where the hem of the jeans must have been twisted tight, like a tourniquet. Below it, the foot was swollen, blue-white. A flap of dead-looking skin hung over a small, darkish hole beneath the ankle; as he watched, sticky, dark purple blood began to trickle out slowly.

'Oh, God,' said Iz. 'That is rank. Shouldn't we patch it up, somehow?'

Helen leant across him.

'Gross,' she said definitively. 'It was swollen before, but I didn't see the hole. Must have caught just one tooth. The blood supply was cut off by the jeans, so it didn't bleed. In a minute, that'll gush everywhere. I bet that hurts now, doesn't it, Johan?'

'A bit,' said Johan, through gritted teeth.

'Nothing to bind it with,' said Helen. 'Anything would do. It really needs a good clean. That water can't be healthy.'

'Infected with crocodiles, very bad for the health,' agreed Iz.

'Use my T-shirt,' grunted Johan, clasping his thumb over the flap of skin in an attempt to stem the flow of blood, which was now flooding over his foot and forming a small, bright pool on the ground.

Helen looked doubtfully at him.

'It's filthy and soaking. And you shouldn't get cold,' she said.

'Mine's dry enough,' said Chris, tearing it off and passing it to Helen. 'If it won't rip, just tie the whole thing round.'

'God, it's an expensive one,' commented Helen, taking it

from him. 'Your mum will go mad.' Unable to bring herself to tear it, she folded it into a bulky pad and began strapping it to Johan's foot, using the sleeves as ties.

'Look at what it did to his jeans,' said Mia, examining the torn and shredded bottom of Johan's left trouser leg.

'Better that than his leg,' said Chris.

'Well, yes, of course,' said Mia, practically.

'Iz,' said Joe, draping his arm around his friend's shoulders. 'Crocodile wrestling.'

'Yeah, I thought you didn't want Joe's hands-on approach,' said Chris. 'Great idea. Not sure it was in the plan, but – you seemed pretty good.'

'Just starting to get the hang of it,' said Iz, spitting again, to Helen's disgust. 'Shame it gave up like that.'

Mia walked down towards the bank, picked something up, and returned to Johan's side.

'You dropped this,' she said, holding out the skull.

'Why, thank you,' said Johan, pulling himself more upright, and taking it from her, 'the cause of all the trouble. Wouldn't want to forget it.'

'Can we move further away from the lake now?' asked Helen. 'I want to be out of its running distance, whatever that is.'

She glanced over towards the distant haze.

'Well, the blur's not gone. Where are we supposed to go now, Johan?'

'Well, now we have the skull, this is surely the end of the road. I think you get to go back now, get out of this dimension. But first, if I'm not mistaken, there'll be a treat for you.'

His voice, they noticed, turned a little wistful. Joe handed him his trainers. He pulled one on to his good foot and stood up, hopping awkwardly with an arm around Joe's shoulder. Joe passed him the other trainer, and Iz, somewhat gingerly, put the skull into his other hand. They stood back and watched him, anxiously. He took a careful step with the heavily padded foot. It took his weight, and he nodded appreciatively at Helen. Then he looked away from the lake, towards where the house might have been.

'Ah. There they are. Last doors, I promise.'

They turned and looked. There was the blur wall, surely a little closer than before. But – were those *doors* in it? Wooden doors?

CHAPTER EIGHTEEN

Curious to investigate, and keen to get away from the lake, they started to hurry towards the doors, but had to stop and wait for Johan, who was hampered by his injured foot. He waved away their offers of help, hanging on tightly to the skull but allowing Joe to carry his spare trainer.

As they approached in the cold moonlight, they could see that the doors seemed clear, solid and as real as anything, though set into the hovering vagueness of the blur. Johan stopped abruptly a short distance away; they paused next to him, gazing at the doors, cautious, hopeful. There were five, all in a line, a metre or so apart, and they were of very old, dark wood with small ceramic handles.

'They're like the doors at the house,' said Helen wonderingly. 'In fact, I'd almost swear they *are* the doors in the house. Like the ones to our bedrooms.'

'And this is where we say goodbye,' said Johan. 'I can go no further. These are the doorways to your possibilities. You'll get your own room, a good night's sleep. You'll wake up back in the house, and everything will be normal. Well, normal but different, I suppose . . .'

They turned to him, concern showing on every face.

'But you are coming?'

'Why do we have to say goodbye?'

'How will you get back?'

Johan waved a hand at them.

'I will be fine. I'll be at the house when you wake up, I promise.'

'You're injured – we can't possibly leave you here,' said Helen firmly. The others nodded.

'This is very awkward,' said Johan, rubbing his forehead and looking everywhere but at them. 'I *can't* come with you. It would be lovely. But I lost my opportunity, when I didn't come as asked, a year ago. I've had my visit to my room of possibility in any case, before that. Now I have forfeited the right, at least for the time being. There are only five doors. One for each of you. Go.'

'What is inside? What do you mean, possibilities?' asked Iz.

'A little piece of a future which could be. It's not the future itself; it may never happen. It's just showing you a little slice of time in your life which is currently, potentially, possible. The design might change on the way there, though – it depends on decisions and events which have not yet happened; the decisions of both yourselves and others. Most importantly for you right now, there'll be somewhere to sleep at the very least.'

Iz looked at him, perplexed.

'Can't you come with me and, kind of, stay over?'

Johan shook his head.

Helen seized his hand.

'Come with me, Johan, come and just try.' She gave him

a little pull towards one of the doors, and, unbalanced, he staggered slightly after her. 'You could just see what happened if you looked in the door – what is it?' She had heard Johan give out a little hiss, as if in pain, and she looked at him in alarm.

Johan dragged his hand from hers. The moonlight bleached the tan from his face, and his eyes, glittering dark, looked hunted beneath the blue shadow of his brows.

'Is it your foot?' Helen put her hand to her mouth. 'Oh, I'm so sorry. Sit down.'

But she needn't have spoken. All the life seemed to ebb from him, and he crumpled down and sat cross-legged on the dark grass, holding his head in his hands.

'You shouldn't have pulled him, Helen,' said Mia matter-of-factly.

They gathered around him again and squatted down one by one. Johan had started to shiver. Iz put his hand under Johan's chin and lifted his face out of his hands. Beads of sweat had started to form on the moon-washed skin. Johan did not look at him. He kept staring past Helen.

'It's a fever,' said Chris. 'I'll bet that wound is infected.'

But Iz had seen fear in Johan's eyes.

'What is it?' he muttered low to Johan. 'Is it the doors?' He trusted Johan now, he realised, but . . . 'What's behind them? Is it really OK?'

'It's not the doors,' Johan said.

Joe, crouching next to Iz, looked at Johan and saw the eyes of a frightened animal. He followed the line of their gaze. He caught sight of something small, sparkling on the ground near the door Helen had been heading towards, and got to his feet. He wandered over to it, kicked at it.

'What is it?' asked Helen, following him.

'Oh, nothing. I thought it was what was bothering him, but it's just a bit of litter.'

Helen bent down and snatched it up. She looked over at Johan. He had stopped shivering and stared at her mutely. She stamped her foot.

'*Damn*, Johan! I can't *believe* this is all it is. For Christ's sake, how long ago was it – how long does it take? See here, I'm screwing it up, it's all gone.' And she crumpled it in her hand.

Iz shot to his feet.

'Here, let me see that.' As Helen's fingers uncurled, he saw what looked like part of a chocolate wrapper. He took it from her and unfolded it gently.

'Foil,' he said, puzzled, then looked at Johan and spoke soothingly. 'It's just a bit of foil, Johan.'

He looked more closely. Before Helen had crumpled it, the foil had been neatly folded.

'Oh,' he said, then angrily, 'Oh. I see.' He closed his eyes. 'Johan, you complete . . .' He seemed lost for words, then gathered breath: 'You ramble on about people, and nets, and turning into glass. Why don't you just talk like everyone else? Why didn't you just come out and say you were a—'

'Because he's not like everyone else!' shouted Helen, rounding on Iz. 'Shut up! What do you know about it anyway? And he's not, not, whatever you were going to say, any more. Are you, Johan? And he never was, for very long. He realised quick and got out of it. Unlike the sad retards you're talking about. That hang around at my house.' She faltered on the last words and Iz looked awkward.

'All right, all right! There's no need to go on at me. I'm just – I don't know,' he said, screwing the foil up into a tiny ball and throwing it hard, far away.

'Disappointed?' said Johan, pushing his hands through his hair.

'Well, yes, maybe, I suppose,' said Iz. 'And maybe a bit hurt that I wasn't let in on this information.'

Helen's eyes flashed fire at him in the darkness.

'There weren't exactly any private conversations on this little trip, Iz. I only heard the same as you. It's up to you to understand. Or not. You never give people time. You never *listen*.'

Iz took a slight step back.

'I–'

But Helen turned furiously to Johan, her hair a cold, angry halo.

'And why are you hiding your face? Why don't you stand up for yourself, Johan? You've nothing to be ashamed of. A bit of old litter reminds you of a bad old habit.' Suddenly, she grabbed one of the long sleeves of her T-shirt and wrenched it up. She did the same to the other.

Johan groaned slightly and put his head down into one of his hands again.

Helen thrust one of her arms towards Iz.

'There! Are you disappointed? Are you?' And as Iz backed warily away, 'Look, look properly.'

Cautiously, he did as he was asked. There were long lines, patterns, scars, running along the pale skin, the length of

222

the arm, some reddish, but mostly silvery white in the moonlight. Iz wondered what to say.

'Crikey. How did you do that?'

'I cut myself.'

'Well, I can see that. I meant, what on? Did you put it through a window?' It was the sort of thing she would do, he knew, with her temper.

'No,' said Helen, speaking with exaggerated patience. 'With a knife. With a compass. With a nail. With whatever was handy. On purpose.'

Iz gazed at the arm, then the other, which Helen was holding forward for inspection. He looked from the scars back into Helen's eyes. Big, blue. The fire had gone from them, damped out by the water which swam there. He put his face very close to hers. He spoke in a low voice, pronouncing each word very clearly.

'And why the flipping heck did you want to do something as stupid as that?'

Her eyes held his squarely. She answered him in the same tone.

'It – seemed – like – a – good – idea – at – the – time.'

'Ah.'

There was a pause. The others watched them, standing very close in the moonlight. Then Iz turned away and Helen rolled her sleeves down calmly, as if nothing had happened. She walked over to Johan and squatted down next to him.

'Very brave, Helen,' he said. 'Good for you, and for me too. Thank you.'

'No, thank you Johan. I shouldn't have shouted at you. I

suddenly realised I was shouting at myself, really. That foil though, that was a coincidence?'

'Maybe nothing is accidental. Doesn't matter. It was all to the good, in the end.'

Joe wandered over to Iz, who was standing with his back to the others, scuffing at the floor with one foot.

'What the hell was all that about?' said Joe. 'It was like a flipping duel. At the end there, I thought you were either going to hit each other or—'

'Did *you* get what he was on about, before? When he was explaining his little problem?' said Iz suddenly, turning to face him.

'Not exactly. But then, I'm used to not getting things. I got the sort of idea. I thought he meant something like that, maybe like, depression, you know.' Joe looked awkward. It was his turn now to look at the ground and scuffle with one foot.

Iz realised Joe was thinking about his mother. He felt inexplicably guilty. Helen seemed to think that if he criticised Johan, he was criticising her. Now he felt like he'd been having a go at Joe's mum, too.

'Depression is one thing. But *that* rubbish . . .'

'People who go a little bit crazy, they want to get out of it, Iz. Maybe they drink, maybe they take tablets, medicine. Some the doctor gives them, some they get themselves.'

Helen was behind them now.

'And sometimes they slice themselves up. It's all painkilling in a funny kind of way,' she said gently.

Chris called across to them.

'Mia says, have you finished shouting and talking, because she is very tired and would like to go now.'

'Coming, right away,' called Iz.

They gathered around Johan.

'You'll excuse me if I don't get up,' he said, looking up at them with a slight smile. He looked much more like his old, boyish self, they thought. 'Just get yourself in through a door each. No more messing about. Do as you're told for once.'

They sensed now that there was no more arguing with him.

'I'm tired too. I'm going to nestle down here for a while. I'll see you all in the morning. Now let me go to sleep.' He lay down, curled round on the ground like a dog.

' 'Bye,' they said, one by one. He flapped a hand at them. He was already closing his eyes.

They lined up in front of the doors. No one squabbled about which one to choose.

'All together?' asked Helen, looking either side of her, at her friends.

'Always so flipping organised, Helen,' said Iz, next to her.

'Yeah,' called Chris from behind Joe. 'By rights, Iz should barge through his first.'

Iz peered around Joe at Chris, and gave him a grin.

'All together it is then,' he said. 'On three. Ready? One, two, three . . .'

And they each seized a door handle, turned it, and opened the door.

CHAPTER NINETEEN

Helen took a tremulous step inside the door. She was in a small, square room decorated in pale colours. It seemed to be some kind of lounge, because there was a fashionably crumpled pale sofa almost in the middle, and a matching chair, facing a small television. It was lit by a side-light on the wall. She felt as if she was invading someone's home, and at any moment they would appear and ask what she was doing there.

But she remembered what Johan had said, and took another step inside on to the thick blue carpet, shutting the door firmly behind her, letting out a breath she hadn't realised she was holding.

There was a window covered with a slatted cane blind on the other side of the room. She walked across to it curiously, parted the slats and peered through. She thought she heard the faint sounds of traffic, of evening people's laughter, but she could only see a blur. She let the blind go, and turned to gaze around the room again. This time her eye caught the corner near the window, where there was a sort of half-height wall dividing off the kitchen area.

It was very small but there were little blue cupboards, a newish cooker, a little sink, a small window of its own. It was all spotlessly clean. Helen forgot her shyness and began to gently pull open doors, drawers. In the corner she found a fridge, with fridge magnets holding on scribbled notes, a postcard, a photograph. Feeling again that she was spying, she stared at the photo. She saw a laughing bunch of twenty-something girls, out in the evening, tanned and dressed up to the nines, in what looked like some foreign outdoor bar. She stared more closely – one of them looked familiar. Disbelieving, she recognised herself. She looked at the photograph for some time, before she gave herself a little shake and looked at the notes. Phone numbers, people's names – what about the postcard? She pulled it from its magnet. Goa. Where the hell was that? She turned it over. It had her name on it, though she could not read the address because the ink had smudged. There was a cheery scribbled note from someone called Rachel who thanked her for recommending the place they were staying at and did she remember that bloke they met in New Zealand, because they'd bumped into him again. She didn't say who 'they' were. Helen placed the card back carefully with a shaking hand.

She wandered out of the kitchen, feeling more confident. She had seen another passageway leading from the other side of the window. This she followed down to a very small but very smart grey and white bathroom, which had everything in it she could want. There were even bottles of shampoo and bath stuff; they were unfamiliar, but when she looked closely, she recognised brand names.

Around the corner from the kitchen area, there was yet another little passageway, with two doors leading off. She peered inside one. It was small and seemed unused, empty except for a built-in cupboard and a folded-up guest bed in one corner. Still, it would do for the night. She closed the door and opened the other. This was larger, with a big window, light fabric hanging from it in great swathes and a big, white wooden bed with linen bedding in Wedgwood blue; a matching side table, a lamp casting a soft welcoming glow. Even a pair of slippers. She opened the door of a fitted wardrobe. Inside were smooth, expensive looking clothes, mostly grey, black and white. She fingered them in awe. Very, very nice. Very smart shoes on the floor. And these, these bright and shimmery things must be for going out. She stroked them silently and closed the door.

Helen felt exhaustion swamping her. She smelt the clean smell of new washing. She wanted to go to sleep. But first, she thought, first a cup of tea in one of the pretty spotted cups she had seen in the kitchen, drunk on the comfort of that sofa. No ironing. No dropouts coming round to hang out with her mum. No kids. No noise. No one else.

*

Mia entered her room confidently. She closed the door behind her with a satisfying click and gazed around. There was nothing wrong with it, no, nothing at all. She liked the calm colour. She liked the minimalist design. She investigated a shiny, polished dark table like marble near the window. It was covered with big sheets of paper which had some kind of blueprints drawn on them. There were pleasingly neat rows of pens in holders, drawers which pulled out, full of papers.

She investigated one of the designs closely. Interesting. She moved on, from room to room. It was a whole house. She found a room which played beautiful music all by itself when you went in, and swirled a fantastic light show around the walls and ceiling, gentle oily blobs which broke apart, joined up again, changed colour. She retraced her steps to a previous room where there had been a simple bed and a duvet. She pulled the duvet from the bed and took it down to the pretty room. She wrapped herself up tightly in it, and lay down for the night, surrounded by music, gazing at the ever-changing patterns around her until her eyes became heavy.

*

Joe stood in the room he'd entered and let out a sigh of relief. It was very nice, very comfortable, very – homely. Not posh or anything, not like the bedrooms at the house, but just his type of thing. Small maybe, a bit cluttered, but everything you needed. The furniture looked like it had come from all over. An oldish, comfortable sofa. A wooden garden chair, painted up, near the window, in front of a big old workmanlike wooden desk with a phone on it, and a clutter of books and magazines, pens and papers. There was a half-decent TV, he noticed, and other doors leading off the room. It seemed to be a kind of flat, he found as he investigated. One door led to a kitchen, where it looked like someone had made the cabinets out of wood themselves. They weren't slick, like ones you saw on television or in other people's houses, but quite a nice job they'd made of it, he thought. He found a bedroom, basic, clean. This was tidier, with laminated posters, mostly of big cats, up on the walls. There were photos, too, stuck on the inside of the door. One of a tiger, and a man playing with it. The man looked a bit like his dad, but younger, taller. He took a step back in shock. It looked a bit like him – but it couldn't be. He turned to another photo. Two women, laughing at the photographer, in a garden. One – crikey, it looked just like his mum, but she seemed younger. The other was just a teenager, maybe. Now she did look a bit familiar. A bit like his mum. Very like his little sister.

Mulling it all over in his head, he prowled back to the lounge area. So many books! He didn't bother with books, usually, with his reading being such a problem. These all seemed to be about animals though. They looked quite good, though most didn't have enough pictures for his liking. He headed on to the kitchen, hopefully. It felt like it had been years since he'd had a snack. Maybe there would be something to have before he went to bed. He definitely remembered seeing a kettle and a toaster.

*

Iz had bounded around the rooms of what seemed like a huge, light house in record time, feeling like a burglar. Now he stood in the middle of the first room he'd walked into, confused and rubbing his head. Like Helen, he couldn't shake the feeling that the owners would come back at any minute and shout at him. It was a lovely house: expensive by the feel of it, but a bit untidy. There were kids' toys all over the place; he'd nearly broken his neck on a Slinky Dog someone had left on the stairs. He'd investigated the double bedroom, where there were soft, smart suits and slick shirts in the wardrobe on the man's side. As he stood, puzzled, his eyes caught the key fob of some car keys lying on the polished coffee table he'd banged his shins on earlier. Slick car too, then. He groaned. There had obviously been a mistake. They should have been told which door was theirs. What had Johan said? 'The door to a room of possibilities . . .' or something. This wasn't his. Oh hell. Chris. It must be Chris's. He wondered if Chris had his now, or maybe they'd all got mixed up. He opened the door he'd come in by, but the blur had sealed across the outside. Oh well, sorry, Chris, looks like I'm here for the night and you are wherever you are, he thought. He shrugged, relaxed. It was a nice place to stay, anyway. Good taste. Everything he wanted. He wandered into the huge, cream kitchen, where everything was irritatingly hidden behind matching unit doors. Eventually, he found the fridge behind one of them, and pulled out milk. Children's blodgy paintings were stuck all over the place. They had started on a cork board, he noticed, and had taken over from there. He filled the kettle, after battling with a rather complicated high-tech tap system, and gazed at the cork board while he was waiting for it to boil. There were sticky notes with phone numbers on, a shopping list and – and one with his name on it.

'Iz,' he read, scrawled in red felt pen which was running out, by the look of it. 'Gone to get Jack from karate. Don't forget parsnips. See you later darling.'

He stood, gazing at it, mesmerised, for a long time. By the time he'd found the coffee, he had to reboil the kettle.

*

Chris had clapped his hands and whooped when he walked into his room. Wow! State-of-the-flipping-art, he thought, as he moved around the gleaming surfaces, the white furniture, the chromed sound-and-audio system he couldn't understand, though he fiddled with it for a while. He wandered the bare, polished stone floors from room to room. He couldn't see anything out of the windows, but it felt high up. An apartment, he worked out. There was no clutter. He found one book. It seemed to be some kind of important novel. It had a plain grey cover. He tried to read a little of it but found it at first confusing, and then rather dull. While the water was boiling in the kitchen in some kind of gadget he couldn't honestly call a kettle, he poked around, but there was nothing else. No photos. No notes. There was a phone which didn't dial out – he tried, just for fun. It did have one message on it. A man's voice said, rather automatically, 'Hi, Chris, I know it's late but we have a problem again on the five zero system. See you as soon as possible.'

He wondered if the others had heard his whoop. He wondered if they would hear him now, if he called to them. He couldn't bring himself to try. Unable to find anything resembling coffee, he tipped a fashionable-looking packet of some kind of powder (claiming it made a refreshing drink when mixed with hot water) into a metal goblet, which was all he could discover in the way of cups.

He sipped it, grimaced, and unsure of what else to do, padded off to bed, in a futon arrangement on the floor of one of the rooms. It was rather hard, and the duvet was too thick and hot, but, overcome with tiredness, he eventually managed to fall into an uncomfortable sleep.

CHAPTER TWENTY

Miss Ermine awoke to the jabber and chatter of excited voices from the rooms either side of her. She listened to the thud of feet; then the deep boom of the boys' voices mingled with the girls' on the other side of the connecting door. She sighed, pulled herself out of bed, and dragged on her dressing gown. She opened the door and put her head into the room. Sure enough, Iz and Joe were talking ten to the dozen at Helen and Mia, who were sitting on their beds in pyjamas, trying to get a word in edgeways from time to time, but laughing a great deal.

'Absolutely no males in the female bedroom at any time, please,' she called.

They stopped talking and turned to stare at her.

'You!' they said, almost simultaneously.

Miss Ermine pulled her dressing gown more tightly around her neck and frowned at them.

'What? Of course it's me. Who did you expect?'

'No, *you*!' said Helen accusingly. '*We* know! Slipping about here and there.' She wagged her finger, but Iz interrupted her.

'Half-scaring to death silly girls that don't know a mouse or a rat when they see one . . .' He ducked as a pillow sailed at his head.

'Oh,' said Miss Ermine, losing her severe look, 'you know. Well, *I* wasn't going to let on if *you* didn't. Sneaking off into the Professor's room the moment you got the chance . . .'

'But you disappeared!' Helen shrieked. 'You abandoned us. Me and Mia had to track down Iz and Joe, and then . . .'

Miss Ermine was smiling now. She held up her hand.

'I didn't want to get in the way. But I never abandoned you – I just, um, became rather small. Forgive me for worrying, for keeping an eye on you.' She looked across at Mia.

'That's all right,' said Mia magnanimously. 'I didn't understand, at first, when the others were talking about it. Stoats. Miss Ermine. But then, sometimes, it felt like it feels when you are next to me. And that was why.'

Miss Ermine smiled at Mia.

'Good. I so hoped it would. And I'm sorry I frightened you, Helen, but you were hurtling straight towards where the mother cat had hidden her cubs – she wouldn't have let you get away with *that* without a scratch.'

'Thank you,' said Helen humbly. 'I do feel stupid now.'

'Not at all. You had reason to run. You were all very, very brave. If you hadn't felt fear, you *would* have been stupid. Now, everyone, you realise how today goes, don't you?'

They looked at her, uncertain.

'Well, we need to do the day of the tour again, I think,' said Miss Ermine. 'They'll only take everyone to bits they didn't see on the first attempt, so people might feel a bit oddly like they've been here longer than they think, but they won't actually see the same things. It'll be a very short tour as a result, and will mostly be to see the skull, which people are so excited to see.'

'I can't believe that'll work,' said Iz. 'I mean, we seemed to be away for ages.'

'You'd be surprised,' said Miss Ermine, 'but it does rely on you lot playing your part. Look out for each other slipping up. But if any of you do decide to start talking, they'll probably only decide you've had a touch of the sun or something.'

'We'll be all right, won't we?' said Helen, looking around at the others.

Mia nodded firmly. 'If I forget and make a mistake, it won't matter. People will just think I'm being weird,' she said.

'Chris,' said Iz suddenly, 'I wonder how he'll manage. It's odd for him. He's not here with us.'

There was a tap at the half-open bedroom door and Chris looked in.

'Ah, you're all here. Thank God. I don't know why.' And he stood in the doorway, suddenly awkward.

Iz beckoned him in.

'Shut the door, shut the door, mate, come on in here. I was just saying, you would feel mad on your own. Who were you with?'

'Charlie,' said Chris, smiling, relieved at the welcome. 'He didn't wake up. It did feel weird. I thought I had gone a bit mad, yes, actually. At least you could talk to each other. But I knew it was all real. I had my wet jeans on and everything. Johan must still have my T-shirt.'

'Johan!' said Helen, remembering. 'I wonder if he's all right.'

'I wonder if he made it back,' said Joe. 'Maybe he died of exposure or something out there.'

'Too warm a night for that,' said Iz confidently. 'He'll be all right. Do you know, Miss Ermine, being – you know, one of them?'

'Iz, do you mind?' said Miss Ermine. 'We spend our lives trying not to stand out. I don't know what you make it sound like . . . anyway, no, I have no more knowledge than any of you. Once I saw you through the doors and knew you were safe, I was off to my own bed. It was far more tiring than I'd imagined. I'm going to get dressed now. Fill Chris in on the details. And I know you might want to talk about everything, but you're going to have to put a lid on it until you're all alone together and very, very, private.'

And she stalked off into her bedroom and closed the door with dignity.

In half an hour, they were downstairs eating a familiar, but nonetheless welcome, fried breakfast. They grew used to the comments of their neighbours that the place almost felt like home, that they felt they had been here for ages already.

There was no sign of Johan. Iz and Helen shot glances at David and Gwyn, eating with the staff at a separate table, but they couldn't catch their eyes.

As the last plates were being mopped with toast, David got to his feet.

'Now, everyone, just a quick look round because I think you saw pretty much everything on the tour before bed. I'm afraid Johan's group will have to muddle in with Gwyn's, if that's all right, because Johan has unfortunately injured his foot.'

He looked straight at Iz's table as he spoke, then glanced across to Chris, sitting further away with Charlie. His eyes were impenetrable.

The tour was short.

They were taken outside, to the walled garden first, to admire the palms and fig tress and the shady lawns. Then, at last, they were back inside, up flights of stairs, and in a dark corridor somewhere at the top of the house.

'The skull is normally locked away,' Gwyn was explaining, in her cool, quiet way, which somehow reached the people at the back of the group without any effort, 'but we have placed it out on its stand for you visitors.'

Miss Ermine, standing next to her, listened with an expression of polite interest.

Those at the front filed past. Helen, Chris, Iz and Joe craned their necks to see. Mia, in front of Helen, waited patiently.

'It's that flipping girl, Trudi,' said Iz. 'She would be in the way. Why is she hanging back? Don't tell me she's scared of a—'

At that moment, there was an ear-splitting shriek. Trudi, in front of Mia, had spotted the skull, and with both arms straight by her sides, fists clenched, was screaming hysterically.

'Flippin' heck,' said Joe, putting his fingers in his ears.

'It's like a car alarm, for Christ's sake,' said Iz, reeling. 'Someone stop her.'

Mia had frozen in front of Helen. Everyone turned in consternation to the shrieking girl.

Suddenly Mia broke away, hurtled past the girl, on down the corridor. They heard the sound of feet clattering down wooden stairs in the distance.

Helen swore.

'Sorry, Trudi,' she said, and pulling the girl round to face her, delivered a sharp slap to her cheek. The sound stopped abruptly, to be replaced by muffled sobs. One of the other girls put her arms around the stricken Trudi's shoulders.

'Are you all right, Trudi?'

'Yes, yes, it's just my nerves. I feel so sick . . .'

Helen bolted past her and paused by Gwyn, who was standing thunderstruck.

'Which way did Mia go?'

'That way. Then follow the stairs down. Miss Ermine went after her. I hope she's all right.'

Helen didn't wait to talk. She hurtled along the corridor. Then, hearing feet behind her, she paused at the top of the stairs. Chris, Iz and Joe were in hot pursuit.

At the bottom of the staircase, they all looked around. They seemed to be back in the original galleried room, with the staircases on either side which led up to the bedrooms.

'I'll bet she went under this one,' said Iz, 'like we did on the first tour. Come on.'

They hurried through the doorway beneath the staircase and along the corridor, past the laboratories. Finally, as they rounded a slight bend, they saw Miss Ermine. Hearing their approach, she turned and put a finger to her lips. She moved aside as they came up to her, and they could see the carved wooden doorway of the Professor's room. The door was ajar.

'Oh no,' Iz groaned.

'Shhh,' said Miss Ermine. She waited and watched.

Suddenly Mia appeared.

She stepped out from the doorway, looked at her feet, looked up and down the corridor, and apparently at them, and then stepped back inside the room. After only a brief pause, she reappeared. She looked thoughtful, then stepped back inside the room. The third time, she looked at them properly, smiled, then began to laugh. In and out of the doorway she went, backwards and forwards, mesmerised as if by a game she had discovered.

Something is changed. Something in me, she thought. Here I am in the room; I can hear the others out there; now I step through the door and I can see them. I won't ever be like Johan, but I do get it. I get it just enough.

'What the hell's she doing?' hissed Iz to Miss Ermine.

'Getting something straight, I think,' Miss Ermine whispered back to him. 'Something terribly important. Changing the way she sees things, getting a part of herself back. When you reach a change in your life, it's like stepping through a doorway into a new world. Mia needs to step through a real one to truly understand. She likes real things, things you can grab hold of, not ideas floating about.'

But it's much more than that, thought Mia, in the Professor's room. I can move in my changed world but I don't lose my own. Not now. Not ever.

She saw the calendar, the crocodile in the glass case above the fireplace, smelt the bitter but comforting scent of the burnt remains of logs which lay within it, sensed the waxy feel of the petals of the flowers they called irises, without even touching them. And she felt the rising bubble of laughter pushing from her chest to her throat, and had no fear of releasing it.

And so they stood, soundless, watching her, until her laughter triggered theirs. Mia held out a hand to Joe, who was nearest; he took it, and as in some kind of formal dance, he stepped with her, into the room, out again, until they were all taking turns, back and forth, back and forth.

As the dance came to an end, Iz, puzzled but smiling, said: 'Now, can we see Johan, do you think, Miss?'

'Of course. Naturally, I know where he is.'

'Naturally,' said Chris, smiling.

They followed Miss Ermine out of the front door, across the brick tracks set in grass between the house and the cottages, and waited as she tapped on the door of the last one.

'It's open,' called a voice they recognised as Johan's. 'Forgive me if I don't get up.'

They hurried in.

He was sitting in an old armchair in the front room, which had a very low ceiling and windowsills crowded with pot plants, and a flagstone floor draped with an ancient-looking rug which had long since lost its colours.

He was smiling and tanned, and looked as if he had had a shower. He was wearing clean, if old-looking, clothes, and his foot, expertly bandaged, was on a little three-legged stool in front of him.

'I'm fine, I'm fine,' he answered to their enquiries after his health, 'I'll be hopping about all over the place tomorrow. We'll get on with some more, um, normal field studies then. Tell me how the skull bit went. Did anything happen?'

'Well, kind of,' said Helen, looking at Mia. 'Though we're not sure exactly what.'

After they had told him, Johan nodded and looked at Mia with interest. 'Mia - you needed something extra, didn't you? Now I wonder - I'm just guessing - but I'd say, you are special. You'll be needed - you have talents which may have to be shared with others. Maybe that wasn't one of your strong points, before?'

Mia gave him a shy smile, shook her head a little, and looked down vaguely at his foot, resting on the stool.

'Is that - well, was that it, do you think?' asked Iz.

'I'm not a forecaster, or really much of a mender of nets,' said Johan. 'If you lot hadn't been with me when I tried to get the skull, I'd probably be munched up inside that crocodile by now. So I'd hate to guess the future. Give it time, all of you. Maybe look for something a little closer to home, a little smaller, instead of aiming for world peace - eh?'

They nodded, content for now. As they turned to leave, Joe looked at the others awkwardly. 'Do you mind if I just ask Johan something - on my own, I mean?'

They looked at him, surprised.

'Of course, you go right ahead,' said Iz suddenly, patting him on the shoulder. 'We'll be just out here.'

They hurried out through the door, and Joe went back to Johan.

'What is it, Joe?' Johan asked. 'Still bothered about Mia?'

'No,' said Joe. 'When you were talking about repairs. For people. And you make bad ones and you make good ones. How - how do people make the good ones? By themselves?'

'Are we talking about you, here, Joe?' asked Johan.

'No, someone else.'

'Someone you care about?'

'Well – yes, I suppose so.' Joe looked at his fingers, fiddled with a bit of nail.

'Can't do it all by themselves. Can't do it for them. So you have to just stick around. Show you care. Don't give up. Don't ask for anything. Drag them around. Boss them about. Be more bloody-minded and stubborn than they are. That's the really tricky part.'

'Oh,' said Joe. 'Well, thank you, that's all right. I can be very stubborn. Everyone says so.'

'Good,' said Johan. 'Now you know how handy that can be. Good luck.'

CHAPTER TWENTY-ONE

Helen picked up her school bag, pushed books into it. She headed for the front door. Her mother heard her and peered out from the lounge. Smoke billowed through the door into the hall. Helen heard the sound of people talking, laughter, music playing.

'Where are you off to?' her mother asked, eyeing her up and down. 'You're not off out, are you? You've still got your uniform on.'

'I'm going round to Mia's. I've got coursework to finish. It's quiet there. I can study.'

Her hand was on the latch.

'But there's the kids' lunches for tomorrow . . .' her mother began.

'GCSE coursework. It's late already. Your kids, your lunches to pack. See you.'

And she was off, out of the door, before her mother could say another word.

*

Iz was sitting in front of the television. His mum kicked at his feet, which were propped on the coffee table.

'Get your feet off, you slob. What are you watching, anyway?'
There was a programme I wanted to see on the other side.'

'Shhh, Mum, I have to watch this for school.'

'Course you do. What is it, anyway?'

'It's for Science. I've missed loads and I'll never catch up
at this rate. Keep out of the way, would you?'

He picked up an exercise book from the arm of the chair
and, unbelievably, started to write in it. Then he looked
back at the screen.

'Well,' she said, almost lost for words. She fell back on her
ex-husband's wisdom. 'All very well. But not a lot of use to
you on the building site, I wouldn't think.' And she took
herself off to her bedroom, to watch her programme on the
television there.

*

Chris was on his way out of the front door, a bulky box on
his shoulder. As his hand was on the latch, he saw his
mother passing down the stairs towards the kitchen, a load
of washing in her arms.

'Off out, Chris? What time will you be back?'

He was about to call out the customary 'Don't know,'
when he paused.

'I was just going to take our old computer round for Joe's
sister. It works and everything – it's a waste, it just sitting
here. Why?'

She paused, looked back at him surprised.

'Well, I just like to know when to expect you. Otherwise
I'll worry.'

Chris took his hand from the latch, and carefully lowered
the box.

'What have you got there, Mum?'

'Just your washing. I couldn't find that nice T-shirt you took on the trip. I suppose you lost it.'

'Yeah, I'm sorry. Actually, I can take this in a minute. It's a bit of a surprise, so they're not expecting me or anything. I'll give you a hand with that, shall I?'

His mother nearly dropped the clothes.

'What?'

'Well, it's my washing, isn't it?'

'Yes, but – you don't know how to work the machine.'

'You'd better show me then. I mean, one day, I'll have to do it myself, won't I?'

And he came back down the hall and took the clothes from her, and carried them through into the kitchen.

*

Joe walked down the stairs from his bedroom and opened the front door. It was a glorious late afternoon. He stood on the doorstep and sniffed the air. Flowers and cut grass. He turned back into the hall and paused outside the closed lounge door. He took a deep breath. He opened the door and walked in. There, in the dark, with the curtains closed, his mother sat, gazing into space, the television on but muted. She watched the silent pictures moving before her eyes.

'Mum.'

She looked up with a wavering glance.

'Joe. Hello. Do you need something?'

'No. But you should come out. Come and look at the day. It's lovely out there.'

She smiled faintly, disappointment wrinkling her face.

'You know I can't,' she said.

'Why? Why not?'

She waved him away, looked down at the floor.

'You get scared, don't you? I know that,' said Joe, advancing and crouching by her chair. He took one of his mother's hands in his. Despite the heat of the day, the skin was cold. She turned and looked at him in surprise. They very rarely saw each other or spoke, let alone touched.

'Have you ever thought,' Joe continued conspiratorially, his face close to hers, 'that it's not fear you feel? It's excitement.' She smiled, looked away from him again, flapped her hand like a shy young girl.

'Think about it,' he went on in a mock-serious tone. 'How does it feel, when you try to step outside? Butterflies? Sweaty palms? Dry mouth?'

She gazed at him, puzzled but still smiling. He seemed to be waiting for an answer.

'Well, yes. And my heart. My heart leaps about like a bird trapped in there. It's terrible. I think it's going to burst out.' Her voice shook.

'Ah, no, Mum, it won't. It just wants to fly. It has to, sometimes. Let's play a game. It's just a game. Come on.' And he pulled her gently to her feet. Resisting slightly but following him nonetheless, she got to the door of the lounge, then the tiny hall. She stood gazing through the open front door in consternation.

'I'm not going out there.'

'No, you're not. Not today. Today we're just playing dare. See, I'm going to get this near to the doorway. You stay there and watch. And now – see, I'm putting my foot over the edge – *it's out over the front step!*' As he spoke, he let his voice build up from conspiratorial to a shriek of excitement. He balanced in the doorway on one foot, and poked the other out as if it might be bitten off at any moment.

His mother gave a little gasp as he shouted and put her hands up to her face. But she laughed, a girlish laugh at the absurdity.

'OK,' said Joe, teetering on one foot for a moment, 'I'm putting the foot down. It's – yes, it's there. One small step for Man; can we see one giant step for Womankind, I wonder?'

He held out his hand to her.

'Dare you!'

She giggled again, then slowly, shakily, held out her hand.

*

Mia stroked the baby's head as it lay in her mother's arms at the tea-table. She pushed another slice of bread into her mouth, and gazed at him as she chewed.

He wasn't so bad, she thought. She hadn't been too keen on all that pink skin at first, but then, she rather liked baby birds and baby rats, and it wasn't so different. She leant over and rubbed her head gently against his face.

He opened his eyes wide at her and seemed to smile.

She put out a finger. He grabbed it and held on tight. She liked that. Proper way to hang on to people, she thought, no messing around.

Her father looked across at her.

'Do you like him, Mia? He seems to like you.'

'He's very good. He's my favourite person. He'll be even better when he can play like a cub.'

'Like a cub?' her mother asked, laughing.

'You know, on four legs. When he can do that. I'm good at that. I can show him. I'll show him lots of things that I can do. And then he can do them.'

She munched the last of her bread in a satisfied way.

The doorbell rang.

'Helen,' said Mia, and jumped off her chair to answer it.

A note from the author

Bettiscombe Manor, a few miles from Bridport, Dorset, has been owned for generations by the Pinney family. It is a beautifully tranquil place, but is famous for the legend of its screaming skull. The story originally claimed that the skull was of a slave. At one point it was thrown in the lake, at another, buried. Both times, it resurfaced by itself. Terrible screams were heard to come from it, and the house seemed to rock on its foundations. This stopped when the skull was returned to the house. Ever since then, it has been kept within the Manor.

With the benefits of modern science, it was discovered that the skull was not that of a West Indian or African male, but of a female and perhaps 3,000 years old. It is believed that the skull came from Pilsdon Pen, the Iron Age burial site nearby.

Bridport itself relied heavily on its net and rope making industry, which still exists today. A happy little town, at one time its name could bring a chill. 'To be stabbed by the Bridport Dagger' meant to be hanged, as the rope for the hangman's noose was made here. My grandmother was a net maker here at 14, and I live in one of the net makers' cottages.